FRACTURED EVER AFTERS

THE DESIRE IN DECEPTION

M.L. PHILPITT

AUTHOR'S NOTE

The Desire in Deception is the prequel to Fractured Ever Afters, telling the story of Lorenzo and Caterina Corsetti, parents to Nico, Rafael, and Aurora from the Fractured Ever Afters series and Hawke from Captive Writings.

This book has content some people may find triggering. You can read the content warning list on the last page.

This book uses Canadian spelling. This means words will have U's in them, "re", or double LL's. (colour vs color, centre vs center, signalling vs signaling, etc.) These are not typos.

PLAYLIST

"Heathens" by Twenty One Pilots
"Gangsta" by Kehlani
"I See Red" by Everyone Loves an Outlaw
"Play With Fire" by Sam Tinnesz & Yacht Money
"Devils Don't Fly" by Natalia Kills
"Lover. Fighter." by SVRCINA
"How Villains Are Made" by Madalen Duke
"Angel With A Shotgun" by The Cab

For those who crave the villain instead of Prince Charming

ENZO

Guns fire and bullets whizz every way, some hitting civilians and soldiers alike, and others narrowly missing. My father grasps my jacket's sleeve and yanks me down to crouch beside him, the tipped-over blackjack table serving as our wall of protection. It's not solid enough for us to remain here long, but it gives us just enough of a reprieve to catch our breaths and decide to escape or fight our way out.

Sweat makes my hair stick to my forehead, so I wipe it to the side. My heart hammers against my chest as adrenaline rushes through my entire body, causing my breath to come out as heavy pants.

I glance over at my father and spot him wiping blood splatter off his forehead. As Underboss, he shouldn't be here right now. Usually, I'm the one who checks the books and confirms every cent coming into our casino remains and doesn't end up in the pockets of our employees. Although they're all extensively background checked upon being hired, one can never be too careful. As Corsettis, the most powerful crime family in all of middle and eastern Canada, our guard *must* always be up.

There is no exception.

But Father insisted on coming today, picking the wrong day to do so.

"It's you and me, boy. *Unisciti a leale. Muori leale.*" Join loyal. Die loyal.

I nod, ensuring my nine millimetre is cocked and loaded. If this ends badly, so be it. Death doesn't scare me, and I don't fear him. He'll welcome me into his fold, even if it's much too early.

Father meets my eyes, and they're hard, as if thinking the same thing. He shifts, readying to stand. The gun shots are slowing as more and more of our men are dropping. When someone barged into the casino and began shooting it up, I couldn't get a clear view of who attacked our own territory admits the chaos.

It might be the Bellinis. A decade ago, Leo Bellini, head of another crime family, and Father had a falling out, and although neither side has ever openly declared war before, it's possible Leo's gotten tired of playing nice.

Either way, after today, war is the only possible future. If Father and I make it out alive, our murderers will pay for their attempt. If we don't, my family will retaliate over the death of their underboss and heir.

Just as my father's positioning himself to stand, his gun cocked, the bullets stop, and everything goes eerily silent.

"Corsetti," a deep voice rumbles. The man's footsteps scuff the carpeted floor as he drags his feet, approaching the blackjack table where we're hidden. "Stand up, you pathetic sack of shit. Letting your men die while you hide is a coward's act."

The line of skin between Father's eyes drops in determination. He's about stand, and while it's admirable to face one's enemy, it'll mean his death.

"Father—"

He slaps a hand over my mouth, silencing my voice, so I convey my thoughts with a pleading look.

Stay.

He shakes his head, his own message clear: *Don't follow me.*

If I were to stand too, we could both die, and as the family's heir, I'm next to take his place as Underboss. Heirdom is everything in the mafia because it ensures there's always a leader to continue the organization and family's bloodline.

Logic battles with honour—something instilled in me since birth. Being a Made Man for the past five years, since I was fifteen, means dying before betraying the family, and to openly allow my father to be slaughtered *is* a betrayal to our leadership.

"Corsetti, I don't have all day," the voice singsongs. "You see, once I take you out, I have a union to go forge."

Father slowly rises to his feet, his arm braced on the floor to help his aging body straighten from behind the blackjack table. Before I can reach for him, he steps away.

"Good, Corsetti. Seems you are trainable after all. Gun on the ground. Now."

From over the table, I manage to peek and watch as Father lowers the weapon to the ground, his jaw tight. The soft *thud* the gun makes hitting the carpet echoes in my heart, matching the desolateness of losing.

"Nice listening," the voice drawls. It's too soft, too mocking, making me want to murder the man simply for using that tone.

"Knees, Corsetti. *Now.* I'm going to kill you as you bow to me. The Bellinis will be so pleased to have you wiped from the earth."

So it *is* the Bellinis behind the attack, even if they're not the one pulling the trigger. Which makes me wonder who the speaker is. Hired outsiders to do what Leo is too spineless to send his own men to do?

Doesn't matter right now though. The only thing that does is the fact that my world is about to be shattered piece by piece because my father sinks to his knees, surrendering.

He's *obeying* him. He's—

"A leader never shows weakness. For a woman, for the family, for an enemy—never."

Yet, by not even trying to fight, he's letting himself be weak.

"Finally, a Corsetti where he belongs." The voice grows louder as he comes closer. "First you, and then I'll find your son. After all, I need to ensure he doesn't touch what's mine. Quite the history your two families have, I must say."

What's going to be his? What history?

"My son will avenge me. The wrath of the entire Corsetti clan will come down on you if you pull that trigger, Rossi."

Rossi. As in...from New York? Why is a Rossi in bed with the Bellinis? Chills travel the length of my spine at the thought of two families working together, against us. The New York *Famiglia* is the most dominant crime family in North American, controlling much of the upper parts of the United States.

"I'll take my chances," Rossi says nonchalantly. "For now, enjoy Hell."

So many things happen in that one second. Things I'll never completely be able to fathom.

Father's eyes cut to me, and I see more emotion in them than I ever have before. Amidst the apology, there's also a fierce fire blazing, begging me to lead in his stead like he's done for all the decades since his own father was taken from him.

I will, Father.

Then his eyes focus back on Rossi—facing his death like a Made Man would.

The sound of the gun going off is loud; more impactful than I ever believed my father's death would be, considering the world we live in. The bullet whips from the barrel and straight into his heart. Blood instantly soaks his shirt, the pool spreading from his chest too quickly to make sense of it.

It's not the first death I've witnessed but it's the only truly impactful one. Common sense weighs my body to the spot, so I don't lunge from behind the table and fight back. My father was correct in that doing so will mean my death as well, and now I have to consider our family. To not break a dying man's final wish.

"Let's go. The boy isn't here. Our intel was wrong, apparently, but we got rid of the head of the snake. Bellini doesn't think the son knows the entire truth, so he'll be less of an issue in the coming months."

Feet—at least a dozen—stomp away, leaving behind the carnage.

I wait until after the door shuts before crawling out from behind the blackjack table and toward Father, where he lies face first in his own blood. With shaking hands, I grasp his shoulders and roll him onto his back. His head lolls to the side, his eyes half open and blank—lifeless. Blood continues to seep from the fresh wound, but there's no point in attempting to stop it.

He's gone.

Along with the dozens of soldiers lying around the room, their own weapons abandoned after they were killed. Scattered among them are richly dressed civilians, who, before an hour ago, were gambling to their hearts content, and our casino staff.

Father and my uncles once told me it's useless to cry over the fallen. People are disposable, whether they're soldiers or family members. Everyone comes and goes; everyone has a purpose. Grieving won't bring them back, so it's pointless to stress about what we can't change.

But before my uncles realize Father and I never returned from the casino, I do cry. In the stuffy silence of the room, with only the dead as my witnesses, I allow the tears to fall from my face and onto his blood-stained cheeks.

The Rossis and Bellinis will pay for this.

Maybe not today, maybe not tomorrow...but soon.

1
CATERINA

6 Months Later

"**Y**ou're so pretty, Cat," Viola gushes. My sister's fingers lightly skate the edges of my veil, as though unable to help herself from touching the gossamer.

"Thanks." My response is absentminded because my mind is distracted, too full of thoughts about my immediate future. Within the hour, I'll wed a man I've only met twice.

Growing up, I always dreamed of a fairy-tale romance. For a handsome prince to sweep me off my feet before marrying me in a lavish wedding and then beginning our happily-ever-after.

But this isn't it.

When Franco Rossi, a member of one of New York's *Famiglia*, proposed a union between our families, Dad was thrilled. It's all I know —all I'm *allowed* to know. Since then, I've wondered what Franco offered Dad in exchange for my hand because that's how this life works. Nothing is free. Marriages are calculated with stakes involved.

"Smile, Caterina," Mom's cold order comes from where she's

perched on the edge of my bed, legs crossed, as she sips from a champagne flute.

I crave alcohol to trick my senses into enjoying the upcoming event, but Mom insists I can't have any. Unless Franco decides otherwise, I'll be limited to one glass at dinner, because somehow, drinking too much on one's wedding day is "unladylike"—Mom's words, not mine.

Using the mirror I'm situated in front of, I plaster on a forced smile. It hurts my cheeks but appeases Mom because I see her nod before she takes another sip of her drink.

We look so much alike, and yet, our differences couldn't be more apparent. Her long, blonde hair is bound in a perfectly styled updo, and her gold dress is impeccable, but her viciousness scares me. Mom's all about marriages and unions; anything to further the mafia bloodlines. She's been like that ever since I turned eight, though I'm uncertain why.

"Better. You should be pleased to have such a prominent match. This will do wonders for us."

Her unspoken words are that the New York *Famiglia* are stronger than us, and if a war were ever to break out, we'd need them on our side.

Unfortunately, this means I have to leave Montreal, the only home I've ever known, and move to New York.

"I am," I tell her, voice fighting not to waver. In the mirror, Viola meets my eyes. Even at fifteen, she comprehends my lie.

It's not that Franco is *bad* or I'm against the entire arranged marriage thing. It's simply that I don't know him. The first time I encountered Franco was when Dad dragged me out to prance—I mean, *meet*— him, which didn't give me much to go on. The second time was at our engagement dinner three months ago. We sat beside each other at one end of the long table, but other men occupied Franco's attention so much, I don't think we spoke more than five sentences to each other.

"Good evening."
"This steak is tasty."
"Cheers." As his wine glass clanked against mine.
"I'm going to speak with your father."

"Good night."

Something along those lines.

Is it bad to want the happily-ever-after? With this life, arranged marriages are an unavoidable reality, and one I was always raised in knowing would be my eventual future. In time, maybe Franco will reveal himself to be my very own Prince Charming. To be the man who adores me and only wants a happy, healthy marriage.

My attention returns to the mirror and the gown Mom insisted on me wearing. It's so over-the-top. It's puffy and sparkly, but the designer claims it'll be ideal for the flowers that were chosen for me. I haven't seen them, but according to Viola, they're another monstrosity designed to lay over the extravagant dress. Imagine Cinderella's ballgown three times over, and it's what they've stuck me in.

The bodice is tied tightly, my breasts nearly spilling out the top. Something else Mom insisted on, which still makes me giggle. My entire life has been about being demure and proper, but on my wedding day, I'm to dress like this. The saying, "they've already bought the milk, so why not buy the cow too?" rings in my ears. Diamonds line the entire bodice, meant to shine in the light. Needless to say, it added thousands to the already-expensive Vera Wang dress.

My hair is in an updo, like Mom's, with chunks of my hair framing my face. My makeup is dark and smoky, but elegant too. I'll admit, the designer who put me together did her task well.

Viola bounces away. Her light blue dress falls to the floor, and she lifts the hem, much to Mom's chagrin. She sneers, watching Viola stride over to the nearest chair.

"Viola, leave your dress alone before you wrinkle it."

Viola rolls her eyes. "Mom, it was just a few steps."

Mom lifts her nose before taking another sip from her flute and glances at the time on her phone. "Your father should be here any moment, so I will take Viola down to get situated with your cousins for the procession. We'll see you soon."

She strides toward me, her mile-high heels making her inches taller than she actually is. She stops by me and leans, pressing a barely-there kiss against my powdered cheek.

"You're lovely, honey. He's a lucky man and you're a blessed woman. Your marriage will be filled with happiness."

She leaves then, my sister following behind her, as her words repeat in my mind three times over.

"Your marriage will be filled with happiness."

There's no guarantee of that.

It's exactly two minutes later when the knock comes, and I take calming breaths while I can. If Mom or Dad spots me freaking out, they'll probably disown me.

"Come in," I call out once I'm partially more prepared for this.

My bedroom door opens and shuts, and I wish the mirror was angled in a way that allowed me to watch Dad enter, rather than me having to turn around. But it isn't, so with much difficulty, I grasp the edges of the gown, lift, and turn the best I can. The weight makes my movements slow and awkward, which makes me question how I'm supposed to walk down an aisle in this thing.

Instead of my father, I'm staring at my fiancé.

His blond hair and blue eyes might be the definition of handsome, but there's something on his hardened face—something dark—that causes my throat to go dry. Instead of a prince, he reminds me of the villain who kidnaps the princess.

Stop it. This will be your husband shortly.

"F-Franco."

My gaze darts to the door and back, concern making the back of my neck dampen. He shouldn't be in here. Grooms shouldn't see their brides before the ceremony, especially not alone. It has less to do with the bad luck myth and more about propriety.

"What are you doing here?" I ask, my voice too thick for my liking.

Franco merely flicks his hair to the side, seemingly uncaring about my nerves as he approaches. "Your father gave me permission."

He did? That's unlike Dad. But who am I to argue with the very man who'll control my life in a few short hours? If he wants to see me now, there's no point in pissing him off.

As though he has the same thought, his attention goes to my dress. His eyes hesitate on my bodice, causing the dampness on my neck to slide down my back, and I shiver, not in desire, but more so in discomfort.

"Fuck, Caterina, you're gorgeous."

His compliment should have me flushing in pleasure. If Mom was here, she'd be falling over herself to ensure I respond appropriately, rather than with the tight smile I manage.

"Thanks."

Franco stops an inch away, his examination of me coming to an end. "Are you nervous?"

What do I say to that? The correct response would be to tell him I'm not, since saying yes may be viewed as an insult.

Instead, I shrug. "Perhaps a little."

Franco doesn't look fazed, just tilts his head in acknowledgement. "I promise to be good to you. You'll want for nothing."

Words that sound pretty, but the missing keywords are noticeable— too noticeable for my brain and heart to ignore. Spoiling me doesn't exactly equivalate to a blissful marriage. Sure, I don't know the guy, so I'm not seeking his love yet, but perhaps something to indicate he'll attempt to make something of us? Promising to be good isn't the same as reassuring me he'll be loyal and will try to create a real loving relationship.

"Sounds great," I respond weakly. My eyes skirt the room again, landing on the door. Dad should be coming anytime now unless he's waiting until Franco finishes his visit.

"You seem uncomfortable, Caterina."

Do I? "Sorry, I guess I'm anxious for the ceremony." Using this as a lead-in, I add, "You should get going. My father will be here to walk me down soon."

Franco doesn't move, doesn't blink. He shows no sign of having heard me. His head simply tilts to the side and his lips purse thought-fully after the longest of seconds. "Caterina, turn and face the mirror."

His voice is cold, abrupt, but I respond instantly with the same ratio-nality as earlier. He's to be my husband soon, so in a mere couple hours, my obedience falls to him rather than Dad. If I act out in public, the family will expect him to discipline me as what they deem appropriate. To ensure he doesn't think me to be a delinquent, I grasp the edges of my gown and manage to lift it an inch. I shuffle in a circle, until I stop, facing my reflection.

Franco's eyes clash with mine in the mirror. He observes me watching him while he lightly touches my hair. So light, if I wasn't seeing it, I wouldn't know he was doing it.

"So gentle. So soft. So demure."

"You seem pleased."

Franco catches a few strands of my hair between two fingers. "I'm fucking thrilled, Caterina. You and I will be in New York by tonight."

So soon? My mouth opens, panic about to lace my response, but I bite down on them. I didn't realize I'd be leaving my home tonight. I'd hoped for a day or two leeway.

His hand lands on my neck, his palm right above my pulse. He can feel my nerves now; there's no denying them. He steps closer, using my neck to pull me tight to his body. The jewelled backing of my dress presses into his tux, and his body aligns with mine.

Other than family, a man's never been this close to me. Dad would kill anyone who tried. My mind aims to remind me it won't matter after another hour, but still, this feels too...too *wrong*.

"Close your eyes," he orders.

I do, hating how I'm trained to obey him, and the moment my sight is gone, his hand shifts, tightening on my neck. I gasp at the intrusion. Panic rises to the top and my hands fly to his, yanking on his grip.

"Hands down," he demands. Softer, he adds, "I won't hurt you."

Hard not to worry when it's not your *breathing getting interrupted.*

For now, I lower my arms, trusting he'll keep his promise to be a "good husband."

"I won't hurt you," he repeats, "in any way that won't be for your pleasure." His whispered words coast over my neck and breasts.

Even being a virgin, his words should spark something pleasurable in my core. But instead, I gulp, and I know he feels it against his hand.

"By tonight, you'll be in my bed, taking my cock like the good girl you were trained to be. I can't fucking wait until you're on your knees, sucking me down this slim little throat." His hand clenches tighter. "I'm imagining you choking, drool dripping, as you try to take all of me. And then I'll claim you in every other available hole you—"

His words cut off, a gurgle replacing the end of his sentence. Something wet sprays against the back of my neck at the same time his hand falls away. My eyes open to catch his body slumping to the floor, blood leaking from a slice on his neck.

But that's not what's most horrifying. Rather, the figure standing behind me is.

He grins a smile of death and flicks his switchblade closed. Bright green eyes find my horrified ones in the mirror, and his smile grows wicked.

"I will confirm, *Kitty*, you will not be sucking his cock tonight since your mouth will be filled with mine."

2

ENZO

When a woman fears me, it makes me excited. Her blood pounds harder, allowing her orgasm to be intensified. Her scent changes, and for a hunter like me, my cock thickens knowing I affect her so. When a woman is scared, it's because she knows her place—which is under me.

And that's exactly what Caterina Bellini feels as her mouth gapes open. Blood seeps into her pristine white wedding dress that's entirely too large to be humane. No doubt, her mother wanted to play up the Quebec Princess title the media coined her, for her American fiancé.

Instead, she's to be my captive. Time to witness the princess beg like a commoner and grant me what I was once promised.

I drag my eyes away from her and toward the piece of shit at our feet.

Franco-fucking-Rossi. Also known as the fucker who murdered my father on Leo Bellini's order. He said as much in the casino, but it wasn't until after my father's funeral, I finally asked my uncles about Rossi's words. There's a truth that was kept from me, and it was time for it to be revealed.

"Bellini doesn't think the son knows the entire truth, so he'll be less of an issue in the coming months."

"Why...What did you do that for?" she asks.

Because your father put the hit on mine. It's only fair I wiped out the asshole who pulled the trigger.

What my uncles admitted cleared up several childhood questions I once had. Even though they encouraged me to leave it in the past, knowing I was nearly a king made it too difficult to forget, especially when I had the ability to pay Bellini back.

Kidnapping Leo's daughter and murdering Rossi will send a message. Maybe then, Bellini will understand not to fuck with my future.

Based on the whole frenzied spectacle below—a chaotic scene making it entirely too easy to slip inside, even with beefy bodyguards blocking the main entrances—it won't be long before someone comes for the bride.

"What do you want?"

This time, I heed the question and peer at her, interested in her pathetic reaction. It's sad, really. She was once a spitfire, but she's become a shadow of herself. It's what this life does to women, and without a strong man to pull her out, she'll revert even deeper into the shadows.

Her wide, innocent eyes scan me, bulging with every inch she takes in. I'm larger than Rossi, towering over her, exactly as I had twelve years ago. The tux I'm wearing, to blend in, is strained across my broad chest. I catch her gaze, but there's no sign of recognition.

Shame. But understandable, since she was only eight the last time we met.

I search for any sign of pending hysteria, since after all, I did murder her future husband right in front of her. I nearly allowed Rossi to conclude his revolting speech, if only to see her reaction, but my own stomach couldn't handle listening to his pitiful attempt at making her horny. For fuck's sake, his words were so cringeworthy, they shrivelled up my dick. She should be on her knees thanking me for saving her from the bastard.

"Wh-wh—" She starts, but she never finishes. Instead, her gaze darts to her bedroom door. "I-I'll call my guards. You'll be dead in an instant if you hurt me."

I tilt my head, a measured smile spreading across my face at the hint of fire beneath her icy skin. She's adorable, believing her feeble threat will frighten me. "That so? Then why haven't you already?"

Because she's in shock. Fear keeps her immobile and unable to react rationally.

"What do you want?" she asks again, this time in a stronger voice, and I smile for an entirely different reason.

I kick Rossi's body. "He's why I'm here." Partly, anyway. Father is avenged, and now, it's my turn.

"Well," her throat bobs with her swallow, "you've gotten what you wanted, so leave. Please."

I inspect her throat for a beat longer, noting the spray of blood painting the pale column. I shift, the appearance of her so tainted, so dirty, because of something *I* did goes straight to my cock.

I move closer, stepping over Rossi's dead body, and Caterina immediately flies backward, pressing herself to the floor-length mirror behind her. Her hands clasp onto the edges, holding it for protection.

Cute.

I close the gap between us, stopping only when her gown folds around my legs, welcoming me into her. Even her clothing knows what her body will eventually understand.

Her throat bobs again, and my hand itches to touch—to feel it move beneath my grip.

"Maybe," I whisper in the small space between us, "I'm not quite finished yet. It's what villains do, correct? I murdered the prince, so it's time to fuck the princess in her pretty dress and ivory tower."

"Please..." But her plea dies out. I'm sure there was a *no* attached to it.

My hand snatches the blood-stained part of her gown, and I fist it, hating how she should have been wearing this for an entirely different groom, and then I'm repulsed that I even care.

A fist pounds at her bedroom door, and a voice immediately follows. "Caterina, is Franco still in there with you? The ceremony should begin soon. You're both needed."

Leo Bellini. The bastard.

My hand snaps up, abandoning the dress for her neck, fingers squeezing her slim throat. Frankly, my blade would have been as effective, but I crave holding her delicate life in my grip.

I grip tightly, enough to spark a gasp from painted lips. "Say yes," I command. "Tell him to go away. Or I'll murder him too. Feel like losing Daddy Dearest?"

Her dark irises expand, filling the entirety of her eyes before she nods once, more of a jerk of her head than anything. "Y-Yes, Dad. He's just telling me about my role in New York. Give us another five please."

Five minutes. We need to leave, and it won't be as easy as it was sneaking in.

Bellini pauses and finally replies, "Very well," before his steps fade away.

"Good girl."

Her mouth parts; her breath shudders in her bodice, and she leans into my grip, her panic being replaced for something reckless. She doesn't even realize she's embracing the desire she obviously feels.

I won't burst her bubble by pointing out that Kitty has a praise kink we'll be exploring soon.

I do allow myself to languidly study her though. Her breasts are piled atop her dress, and while they look fucking delicious, it's obvious her parents were determined to see this wedding through—for some reason I wish I knew—and were using their own daughter's body to solidify their chances.

The dress itself is too grand for my taste. Too poofy and jewelled. It's a monstrosity begging to be burned. It looks heavy as fuck, and no doubt, no one considered Caterina's comfort when they shoved her into it. I'm nearly positive she had little-to-no say about it or anything else when it came to today.

I lean in closer. With my hand around her neck, I control her body, angling her head in a way to grant me access.

"Wh-what are you doing?"

My tongue darts out, collecting the dried metallic flavour of Rossi's blood in my mouth, cleaning the worthless scum from her innocent skin.

Her breath trembles, and I smile as my tongue does another circle. Her body grows weighted, and I'm fucking thrilled to already get her *real* reaction, in such a short amount of time. Her head falls to the side, rendering my hand holding her useless. She presses her entire body into me and—

That's when I realize she's fainted.

~

After receiving my text, Uncle Antonio meets me on the front steps of my mansion as I pull up.

He immediately goes to speak, only to stop after seeing what—*who*—I lift from the passenger seat of my Ferrari LaFerrari Aperta. Her dress bunches, shoving chiffon and silk in my mouth. I half debated removing it from her body before stealing her away from her mansion, but ultimately, she needs to be awake when I slice it off her, so she can see for herself that she's reached the end of her fairy tale.

Getting out of her mansion undetected was challenging but not impossible, thanks to the rope I was certain to bring with me. Scaling the side of her house while her limp body was over my shoulder, and clinging to the shadows meant we got away. Everyone was inside already, waiting for the ceremony to begin.

"Lorenzo."

When he uses my given name, rather than the nickname I go by, it's never to say anything positive.

"Lorenzo, what the fuck did you do?"

I step by him, past the giant glass doors propped open for me. "I avenged my father. He can now lie in peace. And I'm getting what's owed to me."

Uncle Antonio's eyes fall to Caterina. "Is that…? Enzo, tell me you didn't kidnap the Bellini girl."

"Fine. I won't tell you then."

I start up the grand marble steps, rather than down to the basement, where prisoners often find themselves. This princess will be getting a new ivory tower to live out the rest of her days.

Antonio doesn't waste a moment before he follows behind. "Enzo, what was in your head when you constructed this disastrous plan? You're going to start a war with both Bellini and the Rossis. You've made a *huge* mistake." Lowering his voice, he adds, "On her fucking wedding day. I should never have told you the truth."

I spin, the heel of my leather shoes catching on the smooth marble. My teeth bare as I lean over her body and toward him, where he stands on a lower step. "This was and *is* revenge, plain and simple. Franco Rossi killed Father, therefore he had to go. He murdered him in cold blood because *Bellini* put the hit on him." Because he feared we'd drag the past up. "Bellini needs to pay for his own stupidity; therefore, he loses his daughter."

I continue walking, noting how Antonio's footsteps no longer follow. After a beat, he calls up the stairs, "What will you do with her?"

He's questioning me again. Anger nearly has me forgetting who's in my arms as the desire to kick him down the stairs becomes too strong. Gritting my teeth, I face him. "Antonio, *I'm* the underboss here. Do *not* question me or my actions. This is my war, and I'll battle my way to the top if I need to."

I walk away, not giving him another opportunity to speak.

3
CATERINA

*I*t's all a bad dream. It's all a bad dream. It's all a bad dream.

If I repeat it enough, perhaps it'll come true. And when I wake up, I'll be in my own bed and Mom and the hairdresser will arrive, ready to begin the hours' worth of effort it'll take to prepare me for my walk down the aisle. This time, I'll smile when I see Franco—alive—and will look forward to the possibility of a future and whatever happiness we'll find together.

What I won't be doing is waking up in an unknown man's presence. The very man who killed Franco and would have done the same to me, if I yelled out to Dad. I won't be who knows where, unsure if I'll ever get to see my family again.

Having been away in Europe at a private secondary school for the past few years, I haven't been privy to the politics between Dad and the other families. Mind you, I'm assuming it's who my captor is. Or some other criminal who's trying to prove something to Dad. Only someone well-trained would have made it past the guards, into the house, and to my room undetected.

Time to see my reality. Was it a dream or not?

I open my eyes.

Like my own bed, a canopy hangs above me. Unlike my pale pink one, this one's black.

Fuck. So, not my room. Which means everything else wasn't a dream. It means Franco is dead, and I'm not at home.

My palms push into a plush mattress, and I hoist myself into a sitting position. Considering the size of my dress, it consumes nearly the entirety of the king-size bed. Franco's blood stains the hem, a reminder of what happened.

I'm not mad, or even sad about his death. He didn't seem like the greatest man, but I'm uncertain if death is what he deserved. I shiver from the emotionless chill of indifference and the stark terror that a man who sliced a person's neck as easily as he did wouldn't think twice before harming me. It's that thought that has my hands clenching around the dress until my knuckles whiten. My shoulders roll, an attempt to loosen the tension, but the anxiety constricting them is too much to work through.

The gleam of my engagement ring taunts me with how today should have gone.

How long has it been since the break-in? My parents or guards had to have discovered Franco's body by now.

I scan the room, searching for anything that can help me. Beside the bed is a nightstand with only a lamp and a phone's charging cable. Beyond it, floor-to-ceiling windows with dark drapes shut the outdoors from the room, not giving any indication of the time of day.

I continue my visual sweep, noting the plainness of the room, until I spot a chair at the other end.

With a person in it.

A person with green eyes, watching me.

Even from here, I spot the angry thunder within them. The stormy green swirls, locking me in place as the man lifts to his feet and slowly stalks toward me.

I shrink back, realizing other than an insane amount of dress, I have nothing to fight him with. Hell, I don't even know how to properly punch a man, without hurting myself, since fighting wasn't taught to me. Dad said that I would always be protected by guards, so there was no point in learning.

But where were my guards today, huh?

The guy continues his tormenting gait, stopping at the bed's low footboard—presumably *his* bed, if the room's colour scheme is any indication.

"S-stay away from me."

His head does that tilting thing again while he watches me, scanning my form as though he can see right into my fear. His expression—his calculating, narrowed eyes and pursed lips—implies curiosity.

"Once—"

"Once?" I echo. My mind goes through years and years of memories, aiming to pick his face out from the busy crowd. But a man who looks like *him*, with eyes as bold as his are, and a face so impeccably perfect, I'd remember. For the past few years, before six months ago, Europe was my home. My school was an all-girls institution, to ensure my honour remained intact for my husband, so it's unlikely I would have met him before.

Hurt flashes in his gaze, but it dissipates as quickly as it arrived. Instead, he demands, "Stand up."

With my white knuckles still tightened around my dress, I do, not wanting to risk his anger and be killed. It's an awkward shuffle to get to the edge of the bed, and even more difficult to pull the layers off behind me. It's a full minute before I glance at the man again, expectant, only to find a smirk pulling at the edge of his mouth.

"Glad you find it amusing." As soon as the words leave my lips, my teeth sink into my tongue. Attitude with his violent behaviour isn't a good mix. "What's your name?" I ask, to distract him from my previous words.

"You'll figure it out."

Not helpful. "Are you a Corsetti? Or someone else?" I list the only other crime families in the area I know of.

No answer.

"Why am I here?"

He shifts. "I'm getting what's owed to me."

His wicked tone doesn't bode well, nor does his calculating gaze. "What's owed to you?" I manage before the lump forming in my throat gets too large.

He's quick. So quick, I don't see him move, but suddenly, his body is lined up with mine, and his hands find my wrists, yanking them above my head until I'm stuck in his grip. My knees unlock to make my body heavier, attempting to pull from his grip, but it doesn't work.

"You are." Warm breath blows over my face.

"M-me?"

Instead of responding, he scans my face, stopping on my hair—no doubt a mess now—before dipping to my dress, to my breasts.

"Did you choose the dress?"

A strange question. I shake my head.

"Do you like it?"

Honesty feels relieving, so I shake my head again. "No. It's too heavy."

His pupils dilate, the green of his eyes becoming so much larger. "This atrocity will come off you. It makes me sick to look at. You will shower, because I refuse to have you when another man's blood is on your skin. From now on, any marks on your body will be left by me. Understand?"

I nod, because how else do I respond? My excitement tampers into a mere stomach flip at the thought of fresh clothing. His other words fade away, fright second to caution.

When his grip around my wrists vanishes and my arms lower to my sides, I ask, "Where can I get changed?"

He laughs. A full-on belly laugh I suspect doesn't come from his sinful lips often. It continues for a minute, and each passing second has my annoyance growing.

Finally, his laughter dies off. "Princess, this isn't a fucking hotel. You don't get that kind of freedom, and you most definitely won't be removing your own dress. *I* will. And then I'll burn the fucking thing."

Franco is gone, so to be honest, I don't care what he does with it, but hearing his transparent words—that *he'll* undress me is…No. It won't happen. This day will end with a shred of my decency still intact.

My chin lifts. "Then I'll stay in the dress, please and thank you."

He laughs again, this time more of a chuckle. "You're adorable, I'll give you that. So polite." One hand disappears into his pants pockets. It dawns on me then, he's dressed as a wedding guest would be, explaining how he got inside my home. From his pocket, he pulls out the same switchblade as earlier. My breath stalls and I wait to see what he'll do with it.

It snaps open, the metal shining and gleaming in the bedroom's overhead lighting, stealing my breath with the action. Franco's blood is still on the blade, and I nearly gag.

"You see your fiancé's blood? I think it's fitting he still has a hand in undressing you tonight."

With a flick of his wrist, his hand carves down. I flinch away from the blade, but he meets his mark and the slice lands between my breasts, catching the bodice, then slips down, separating the delicate cloth.

"That could have been my skin!"

He simply shrugs, his attention not leaving the open area the rip has left behind. "Could have, but it wasn't."

He tosses the knife to the side, and it thumps onto the cushy duvet, but I don't dare look away from him as his hands catch the edges of his handiwork and with little effort, he rips the rest of the dress, all the way down to my waist, baring my upper half. My arms immediately go to my chest, over the low-dipping slip, and cover myself.

"Shame to waste such a lovely dress. I'm sure it cost a pretty penny."

"Something like that."

"If it's any consolation, that fucker didn't deserve you."

"How do you know he didn't?"

Instead of responding, his hand reaches toward me, and I bend backward in escape, my feet remaining glued to the floor. He doesn't stop though, not until his finger finds the skin of my breasts, and he draws a line overtop them.

I stop breathing. Stop thinking. Everything inside me halts in order to watch and wait for that knife to end up in his hand again, where it can easily mar my skin.

His finger continues its journey, edging my own hands until he lightly pushes at them, nudging them away from my body. Like the fool I am, I allow it, and my arms fall limply to the side.

With access granted, his finger explores my skin, leaving a path of flames in his wake. I clamp down on the growing feelings his touch erupts inside me. My thighs clench together but are thankfully hidden by the dress.

His finger shifts downward, following an invisible path toward my stomach and stopping where his slice ended. He grasps the edges and rips the dress down, down, down, until it falls completely from my body.

My arms aren't long enough to cover my entire body, but I sure as hell try, even pulling the slip farther down my hips to conceal more bared leg from his roving gaze.

"Fuck." The curse is so faint, so low, I'm positive he doesn't realize he said it. In a thick voice, he rumbles, "Lie on the bed."

Everything crashes around me. I've heard about it in the media—about innocent women encountering bad men on the streets and they take what isn't theirs; what isn't freely given.

"N-n-no. No," I repeat, firmer, "No."

He jerks his chin toward the mattress again. "Get on the bed, and do *not* make me ask again." His voice drops to ice and I back away, lowering my arms away from my body as I spin, facing the bed. I don't want to risk what he'll do to me, but I sure as hell won't be doing *that* with him.

But then, a signal flickers. On the bed, his blade waits, open and ready for me to stab him. I stare at it a beat longer, noting the blood on it. Can I add this guy's blood to Franco's?

"Get—"

Yes. Yes, I can.

In a move, I'm hoping is quick enough, I seize the blade's handle and spin, shoving it toward his face, stopping short of his cheek.

He blinks slowly, lazily, a smirk growing on the corner of his mouth.

"Not sure what you're smiling at, but you're getting me out of here and back home or this will end up in your heart."

His smile continues. "You've passed my test, Caterina. Stab me. Go ahead. Aim for my heart."

This must be a test too, right? I glance at the spot on his chest I'd need to pierce before slowly shifting the angle of my arm, so the blade is lined up. My eyes don't leave his and I watch, waiting for him to stop me.

He doesn't. The blade's tip presses into his tux jacket, right where his heart is.

"Last words?"

He chuckles. "Get on the bed."

He's kidding, ri— As fast as the thought is formed, the blade is smacked away from my hand, and my body spun around, my back to his front. His muscled arm is yanked under my chin, preventing me from moving, while his other arm locks mine to my sides.

"So, you do have fire in you."

Why am I surprised it was a ploy? His brain functions like a psychopath's.

"Get on the bed and don't think about trying to fight me again." He shoves me toward the mattress, his arms releasing me.

You told me to, dick.

This time, the climb on the bed is easier without the cumbersome dress. My attention goes to where it's on the floor, and he notices right away where my concentration had gone to.

"Missing him already?"

Nope. "I thought you said I'd be showering?" I indicate the dried blood. "You know, to clean this off me."

"Not yet. I have matters to attend to, and you won't be wet and soapy without me here to watch."

My teeth smash together and my hands fist at my sides. "So, what then? I'm to wait here, *undressed* while you gallivant around?"

"Nope." His *P* pops, and the casual sound is distracting. Enough that I don't pay attention to him reaching into the drawer on the bedside table, pulling out a set of metal handcuffs. Before I can even blink or attempt to escape, he has one snapped around my wrist.

"What—no! Wait."

My complaints are ignored, and my other arm shoved into the remaining cuff. They're yanked behind my head, where he clasps them to the bedframe, forcing my body to be stretched out, my arms strained above my head. The pillows beneath me shove my back in an arc, my breasts pointing high to the sky.

Which is where his gaze ends up. His pupils dilate and I swear his nostrils flare. He licks his lips before saying, "You will lie here, handcuffed, while I conduct my business and wait like the good girl you are."

Beneath my heavy breathing and growing panic, my body pauses. Heat flushes my core and I press my thighs together, my mind working to determine what in this fucked-up scenario has my desire surfacing.

He bends himself over me, his eyes travelling to my breasts. He pauses there, and I can almost *see* the debate rolling through them. I shut my eyes, praying he considers me weak, so he'll leave without touching me.

He does move away, and just when I'm feeling victorious, he returns with his knife. The slip—my only protection—glides away from my body, the edges landing on either side of me, baring my naked breasts to him. Thankfully, he didn't cut all the way down, and my thong remains covered.

Cool air pierces my nipples, hardening them instantly with awareness that this stranger—a kidnapper and murderer—is the first man to ever see them.

"That's better."

"Why?"

"Because I can, Caterina. Simply because I can."

He holds the knife in the air, turning it once, inspecting it as he contemplates further. A sour taste fills my mouth, hitting the back of my throat as I wait for the inevitable to occur.

After a second, he lowers the blade to my skin, right against a nipple. Its chilling temperature lines my chest with ice, and if I breathe too deeply, I'm sure it'll nick me.

"Did you know blood swells faster when a person is panicked?" Masked green eyes find mine and beneath his perfect features, he smiles that malicious grin he's so fond of. "So, ease your breathing or this will hurt more."

The sharp point pauses against my nipple. Instead of easing my breathing, I stop altogether. No breathing, no moving, nothing.

"How do you feel, Caterina?"

"Scared." My honest answer is in hopes he'll realize how his actions affect me.

"I can relieve you of that fear," he offers. "Fear for pleasure is a better deal, no?"

My lips part, a question there, when the blade sinks into my breast, yanking a surprised gasp from my throat. Stinging pain instantly accompanies the feeling, and a dot of red trickles from beside my nipple.

"Y-y-you cut me."

The dark stranger watches me, that contemplating look, once again, taking over his expression. Keeping my gaze, he lowers his head, his hair brushing against my collarbone, and that's when I realize, his nearness isn't going away.

"Wait, what are you—"

Lips capture my nipple, pulling tight before his tongue sweeps the area, lapping up my blood.

A betraying moan slips out, my neck muscles too weak to watch as he takes a first from me. The downside of being a daughter to a boss means I'm so overly protected that *everything* on my body is untouched, not just my virginity.

His tongue swipes my nipple again, before he sucks deep. As promised, the pain from his cut melts and is replaced by pure, unbridled pleasure.

I *hate* this. I should *not* be feeling like this. Not for him—for my captor and fiancé's murderer. Yet, my body hasn't gotten the message, and my hips roll, seeking more of the same elsewhere.

But instead, he pulls back and stands, his lips stained red, causing my stomach to lurch in unspeakable ways. His tongue peeks out, licking the rest of me off him.

"Had to ensure the blood stopped."

With the spell gone, anger replaces pleasure. My legs kick out, catching him in the side. The realization that a man, who is *not* my fiancé, had his mouth on my intimate parts, who cut me—the very man who *murdered* Franco—is the very man whose name I do not know.

His hands catch my ankle, his brow lifting. With his large, rough palm binding my leg, it's then I comprehend how thin and breakable I am compared to him; how a gentle squeeze from him would cause my ankle to pay the price. He lowers my leg back down, releasing it only when it's flat on the bed. His other brow lifts in a *don't do it* warning.

When I remain still, he backs away.

"Consider that your first mark, princess."

I lash against the cuffs, feet freely kicking out, though it does nothing but tire my body faster. "What does that mean?"

Silence stretches between us for a long, bated moment until he shrugs. "Guess you'll be finding out, Kitty Cat. Rest well."

The door opens and closes, and he's gone. My head falls onto the bed and an annoyed breath puffs out of me.

I won't be here for long anyway. By now, Dad's had to have discovered what happened and is searching for me. I only need to survive my villainous kidnapper until he finds me.

My arms yank against the cuffs but all that does is shove the metal farther into my skin, rendering my attempts useless. I shut my eyes, closing out the world and willing my mind to slide into a happier place —home and in my own bed—and away from my psycho kidnapper.

Kitty Cat. Such a familiar nickname. Where have I heard it before...?

4
ENZO

I shut my room's door, already typing out a quick message on my phone. Within minutes, Marcus Corrigan arrives. Not much older than me, but his father's worked alongside my own for so many decades, Marcus and I practically grew up together, and I trust him to not to go inside.

"Marcus, stay here. I'm the only person who comes in or out. If you hear yelling or banging, ignore her."

He looks to the door, his mouth curving in a way indicating suspicion. "Would that be the Bellini girl, sir?"

Another guard would be reprimanded, but since it's Marcus, I tell him the truth. "It is. She won't be an issue."

With Caterina taken care of, I head toward the storm below. Antonio isn't one to let things go, and no doubt he's been stewing since I reprimanded him earlier.

As expected, Antonio, along with my other uncle, Tommaso, paces at the bottom of the grand staircase. I pause at the top, an annoyed, drawn-out sigh escaping. If I was Father, they wouldn't be questioning me. Antonio was Father's consigliere, his advisor, but neither of my uncles understand I'm not my father.

Today will be the final time they question me, because from here on out, *I'm* the person ensuring our continuation—am guaranteeing our prosperity and control over the city. I'm working on regaining an empire, and they both need to shut the fuck up and accept the process.

The moment my foot touches the bottom step, Antonio is right there, shoving his finger in my face. I give him a moment, warning him with a single look that if he doesn't lower his hand, I'll be breaking the finger.

The look works, but his hateful glare deepens. "You're stupid, boy. You're chasing a past you were denied and fucking up the present in the process."

Tommaso steps closer, placing himself beside Antonio and signalling who's side he's taking. "He's right, Lorenzo. War with the Bellinis and the New York *Famiglia* isn't worth the gains she'll bring. Bellini will fight to get her back, and New York won't let this go. You murdered one of their own and prevented a union."

And we mafia families *love* our marriages. A single set of vows can create or break alliances.

"If Leo Bellini wants to attack, he dies, which makes this easier. *You*," I jab a finger in Antonio's direction, "were the one who told me what I could have had. What *we* could be right now." If Mother never opened her stupid mouth twelve years ago, I would have been on that alter with Caterina today. "We could have built an empire. Bellini and Corsetti joined together under one leader—me."

Because once Leo Bellini dies, there are no male heirs, so it'll revert to Caterina's husband.

"But that's *not* how it is, Lorenzo; therefore, you fucked up." Antonio sneers, his chin lifting so he can look down on me, despite my taller height.

As much as Antonio's been a second father to me—having completed much of my training himself—he changed once I took over. When he should have become compliant, he instead chooses to frequently defy me.

I do recognize the decision as a bad move. The moment I killed Rossi, I knew it'd be the beginning of war, but the plan had already been put into motion. Once I finish with Caterina, her father will fall in line. And with the Bellinis and Corsettis on one side, even if it's an uncomfortable truce, New York will back down.

"Antonio," I start, using his given name to remove any familial relation between us, "I've already warned you. Last chance. You drop the matter, or you'll find a bullet in your skull."

His skin flushes red, his puffy cheeks causing him to look like a chipmunk. But the idiot doesn't stop. "I'm not letting this go, Lorenzo. Your decision has put the entire—"

His words are cut off when my Glock is shoved into his forehead, my finger over the trigger. Not that I want to kill him, but this truly is the last time he'll be questioning my actions. From the corner of my eye, I spot Tommaso step back, wisely separating himself from the scene. His eyes drop to the floor, his chin going tight.

"It's *underboss* to you, Antonio, and you'd best remember that. Yes, my decision has placed us in danger, but we won't be for long. You trusted my father's choices, and now, you're to do the same for mine. I have a plan, and that's all I'll say on the matter."

Antonio's eyes widen, but the moment his hands come up, palms facing me, I know I've won.

"What are your intentions with the girl?" Tommaso asks, crossing his arms.

I slide my gun to the right, now pointing it at him. "Does it matter, Uncle?"

His jaw clenches, but he lets the topic go with a simple nod of his head. With them both neutralized, I lower my weapon, tucking it inside the back of my pants.

"Now then, I trust you'll handle it if we're contacted by Bellini?" In the five hours since I escaped with the bride, Leo's had to have discovered Rossi's body and has been going insane to determine who's responsible and where his daughter is. At last, he knows a fraction of what it feels like to have one's life ripped away so viciously. He's lucky I need her, or else I'd deliver her head back to him.

Tommaso nods. "I know Leo, and he won't reach out because he'll be waiting on us to make the first move."

I shrug, already briskly walking away from them and this pointless conversation. "Either way, you know what to do. Inform all the guards in case there is an attack and ensure everyone knows not to go near my bedroom or they risk death. Have the kitchen prepare a tray for her and deliver it outside my door in an hour."

Once orders have been given, I stride toward my office because as much as I'd like return to my captive, the business can't be ignored. Ignoring my role opens the doors for fuckers to slide in and take my place. Fuckers like Antonio, who'll easily turn on me if he notices businesses slipping. He'll blame Caterina, claiming I've bit the poison apple, or some shit.

The door to my office slams a bit harder than I mean to with the adrenaline this day hyped up within me. Being alone gives me the space to let out the deep breath I feel as though I've been holding all evening, and as I stride through my office, immersing myself in the deep oak walls and scent of rich leather, the weight of today's accomplishments getting heavy.

After pouring whiskey in a glass, I head toward my desk. The leather creaks as I drop down in my seat, swivelling toward the stack of documents to review—some legal and some less so. The casinos, the clubs, even the tattoo parlours all bring in money. They operate as a way for us to be front and centre to the public and to keep fear alive. Of course, they also serve as fronts for the less legal businesses—weapon trades, drug smuggling, prostitution, as well as dealings with the local motorcycle club, the Hell's Angels.

Head members of the family—other uncles and my father's cousins—oversee each one, but I prefer to have final say on everything. Father delegated and never oversaw their work, which is perhaps why people like Antonio struggle under my new leadership style. I prefer to witness and confirm that the money coming in remains in place and doesn't find its way into other's pockets.

I lift the latest report from one of the strip clubs, finding the profit margins higher than usual and indicating a more lucrative month. I ease back in my chair, sipping on the whiskey, pleased with my progress as leader.

After three more documents, my mind begins slipping away; it has nothing to do with the alcohol, but rather, the woman tied to my bed. It goes straight to the past to when we first met and she was an eight-year-old with a blue ribbon tied in her hair. I recall how it made her eyes brighter, because even at eight, I recognized she'd grow up to be beautiful.

And fuck I was right. Beautiful and so fucking responsive. She's terrified, but her blatant desire is delicious. She responds to me—to the names I call her, to how I control her body. She doesn't fight, which will make my next move more enticing.

I feel my cock thickening, so before it gets to the point of pain, I abandon my drink and leave the office, ready to go unlock my princess from the tower she's found herself tied up in.

After all, that's what villains do, right? Find the princess and steal her for themselves.

5
CATERINA

*K*itty Cat.
     Kitty Cat.
     Kitty Cat.

I've spent hours, my brain repeating the words until they finally come to me. Until they make sense—until *someone* claims them.

Kitty Cat.

Kitty.

Cat.

Caterina.

"Your name reminds me of a cat. Caterina. Like, a kitty cat. Can I call you that?"

The gasp consumes me: mind, body, and soul, as I'm yanked into the past, to a time and a place anyone would have blocked from their memory. Not because it was a horrible period, but because being eight means memories grow fuzzy with age.

I go back to a particular moment, when Mom, Dad, and I spent the summer at our private cabin in Northern Quebec. It's where I met—

"Caterina, I want you to meet Lorenzo Corsetti. He's to be your new friend."

"I prefer Enzo," the young boy counters right away, his bright eyes shining brightly. His hand juts out, the evidence of his father's training in this strict lifestyle. Neither him nor I are regular kids. Just like this isn't a typical way to meet new friends, but Daddy doesn't seem to care when he dragged me away from my other ones in Montreal to meet Lorenzo—Enzo.

I take his hand, shaking it once before glancing at Mommy to make sure she approves of how I'm acting. She smiles briefly before looking at the man standing behind Enzo. Mr. Corsetti is large and scary like my daddy.

"Caterina," Enzo repeats, grinning. "Your name reminds me of a cat. Caterina. Like, a kitty cat. Can I call you that?"

"Sure."

I kind of like the idea of a nickname. Maybe this friend won't be so bad. I've never had a boy as a friend before. Mommy says it's vital to surround myself with girls from other prominent families and to avoid boys until I'm older. I think she doesn't want me kissing them, which, ew. As if I'd try.

The next step in any introduction is to invite them for an activity—for drinks, food, conversation, or in my situation, to play. Mommy taught me that.

"Do you want to go look at the fountain in the garden?" I hike my thumb behind me. "It's really pretty."

Enzo gestures to start walking, and when I do, he falls into step beside me.

The click of a door rips me from the memory, and when the ghost of my past re-enters, I jerk, my feet pushing into the soft mattress until I'm able to shove myself against the headboard, uncaring if my breasts are on full display. With my hands bound, it's awkward as hell, but still, I manage to gain a few inches of distance from him, so it's a win.

He—Enzo—fucking *Enzo*—shuts the door behind him, pausing as he takes me in. I'm sure I look ridiculous, pressed against his headboard, but, like, *fuck*, how else should I be responding?

That summer when I was eight was the first and last time I saw Enzo. When I asked questions, my parents told me life moves on and to forget about him. Did I? Not for a few months, but after a bit, sure. I mean, I was fucking *eight*. My attention span only lasted so long. Enzo became a blip in my life, until I aged, and he became nothing more than a buried memory and the Corsettis returned to being my family's enemy. My parents never told me why we spent a summer hosting them, and once I got to an age where those kinds of questions could even be brought up, the memory of Enzo had long faded away.

"S-stay away from me."

He doesn't. Enzo's slow gait continues until he reaches the edge of the bed, where he stops, watching me with an amused smirk.

"Come now, Caterina. You choose now to find your claws?"

"Nice metaphor," I snarl. "Lines up with the nickname you gave me, *Enzo*."

Surprise flutters on his features so quickly, I nearly miss it. He sits at the edge of his mattress and leans back against the footboard, one leg still dangling off the edge. A casual position, but all it does is spike my nerves.

"You figured it out. Good."

"*Good.*" The scoff burns my throat. "*That's* what you have to say to me. *Good?*"

His arms go wide, his palms up in the air. "What would you have me say?"

"I-I don't know." Breath rattles from my chest, but it's not enough to remove the ache. "Something other than that. I mean, you're a *Corsetti*. It all makes sense now."

Putting aside the shock of who he is, Made Men are one thing— their name. Lorenzo Corsetti is my enemy—my father's enemy—and he interrupted my wedding, killed Franco, and kidnapped me, all to start a war.

"Please explain," Enzo murmurs calmly. "Tell me what you believe is happening here."

"You want a war with my father. You thought kidnapping me would be the way to do it, and Franco was in the wrong place at the wrong time, right? You knew the bride would be alone in her suite, and that's why you came when you did. You want money or something? Power? You want to see my father kneel as he begs for my return." And he *will* do that. Dad loves me, and as the eldest child, he needs me. I can now be used for other alliances. It's horrible to be viewed as meat, but in this lifestyle, that is unfortunate purpose of women.

Other alliances.

"That's it! You stole me so you can ransom my return, and with less money, my father might be unable to find another alliance as profitable as Franco was for us. You know, no matter who my family aligns with, you'll be screwed, and that's what you're trying to stop."

Enzo's features remain flat. So flat, I'd think he didn't hear a word I spoke. After the longest moment, with only my heavy breaths catching up after my winded revelation, he moves, reclaiming the place beside the bed.

I watch, stalking his every step and waiting for him to strike. Frustration burns at my chest when he continues to do nothing.

"Well?"

His lips press together once, and instead of speaking, he leans forward, his chest coming closer. I move away, despite the pull on my wrists. At the last second, he yanks a key from his pocket and slips it into the cuffs. Understanding his actions, I resist wrenching them away.

Finally, the cuffs open, and I immediately roll to the side, off the bed, and away from him, jerking the sides of my slip together, managing to cover my naked breasts.

Enzo climbs off the bed, putting us in a standoff with the furniture separating us.

"That's what you think this is? A way to bankrupt your father so he can't use you to make alliances?" He pauses briefly, the hint of a frown lining his mouth. "Answer me this honestly: how does it feel to know your entire purpose in life is to be a pawn?"

In school, the other girls often spoke about leaving their boyfriends to attend school, as commanded by their influential families, but each of them called their boyfriend in the evening, after dinner. They spoke about returning home on holidays and spending time with them. They recounted their dreams of how after high school, they hoped they'd be able to get married and live their happily-ever-after.

The happily-ever-after life is all I've wanted, and yet, I'm the only person not to receive it. My prince is dead, but Dad will soon find another one for me to wed. And my current companion is my villain, so if that's saying something about my fairy-tale ending...

It's the price of being a woman in a mafia family. The reality is simply that. Women are wed to Made Men. Alliances and friendships are secured. Trade and business dealings increase, continuing the harmonious lifestyle.

Without looking at him, I answer, "It's part of this life." I gesture around the room, flicking my fingers toward him. "You know that."

"Ah." Feet drag against the carpet, pulling my attention from the bed in time to watch his slow pace around the bedframe. "That's not what I asked. You've listed a fact. My question is, do you enjoy it?"

No. But it's what it is, and I wouldn't want to be a regular woman living outside the organization.

He continues, stopping a foot from me, and my hands clench the fabric of my slip tighter, in hopes to prevent his gaze from penetrating my clothing.

"No," I whisper. "But I'll continue doing it."

"Like the good princess you are. Simply hopping from man to man when Daddy commands you to, correct?"

That's not...It's not... Resentment burns the edges of my chest as my cheeks heat. My grip on my slip tightens, knotting in the fabric as I bite down on the multitude of curses running through my brain.

"It's the life," I respond weakly.

"Hm," is all he murmurs before stepping aside. His arm gestures to the opening at the other end of the room. "I told you you'd be getting a shower, so go."

I don't move. "You said I assumed incorrectly, so if not for ransom, why *am* I here?"

"In time, you'll learn."

My teeth grit. "But it's not what I guessed?"

"Not even close. Now go to the bathroom before I carry you there myself."

Darkness settles over his eyes, so before he finds a reason to punish me, I will my feet to move toward the opening across the room. He follows directly behind me, making me feel a bit like prey.

With my back toward him and my face hidden by my hair, I ask, "What happened to the little boy I knew?"

His scoff is so loud it's as though he yelled it in my ear. "The boy you knew?" he repeats. "Kitty Cat, before an hour ago, you didn't even remember who I am, so I'd say you never *knew* me. I was a moment of your past."

The past. The fact is simple but weighted, pulling me to a stop in the doorway of the gleaming bathroom. "But not my present."

His eyes narrow, shutting the green off entirely, and with a flick of his wrist, he shoves at my shoulder. My feet stumble, body falling backward but, thankfully, I retain my balance as we enter the white, marble bathroom.

He continues his pacing, forcing me deeper in the room, and for a second, I'm reminded of Snow White and the Huntsman who stalked her into the forest.

"You're pissing me off, Caterina. Your questions were cute, but now you're bordering on defiant. Be good and remove the rest of your clothing."

"With you here?" It's a question but stated more in a *you're kidding me?* tone.

"Get used to it."

6

ENZO

Like her, my memories of our summer together are faded. Until Antonio told me everything and then suddenly, my ten-year-old self's memories returned. I recall meeting Caterina, shy and pretty. She was so fucking demure—the perfect mafia daughter.

When Father told me to be nice to the girl, to become friends with her, I knew there was more to it, but at ten, I didn't dare ask questions. So, I remained polite as she led me to the garden's water fountain and yapped about how she enjoys the sun shining over the water.

That first day, she was so annoyingly perfect. At supper, she sat beside me and made small conversation. In the evening, she led me to the room her mother had pre-chosen for me.

Over the next week, it was very awkward. I preferred to be in Montreal, exploring downtown with other sons of Made Men, and honing my fighting skills, but after a while, her gentle laughs and excitement at nearly everything felt refreshing.

It's funny how twelve years can change things, how aging separates a person from their childhood.

And we're certainly not children anymore as I prowl through my bathroom behind her. She's walking backward, her eyes locked on me.

Fear is evident in every inch of her, from her scrunched brows to the white-knuckled clasp around her slip.

Caterina's back meets the glass-walled shower, sparking a flinch as the cold glass touches her bare skin. Her head whips around, her hairdo from earlier today a scraggly mess and my hands itch to remove the clips holding the strands in place, to have them tumble down her back like a blonde waterfall.

"Strip," I order again. "We've already established I won't be leaving."

"But you're not telling me why."

Except I have already. "I've already told you; I'm getting what's owed to me."

What was stolen from me before I even had the opportunity to claim it. A chance given and taken away over the course of a three-month summer.

"You said *I'm* what's owed, but you're not explaining what that means."

"Last chance. Remove the rest of your slip and perhaps you'll learn."

Caterina huffs, and the clear annoyance rolling from her is too delicious not to smile at. But finally, she does as instructed.

I avoid moving—avoid informing her exactly how much she's affecting me. For every inch of creamy skin revealed, I feel my cock twitch. The slip falls to the tile floor and her arms immediately cover her breasts, as though I haven't already seen and tasted them. The only thing she wears is the tiniest scrap of silk between her legs, covering her innocent pussy.

A pussy that won't be innocent by the end of this night.

A pussy that'll help me reclaim everything I could have had.

A pussy that'll take my cum and produce an heir.

"Drop your arms. They're nothing I haven't seen before."

Red blossoms across her face and neck, nearly masking the dried and faded blood of her dead fiancé. Her arms drop to her sides as she reveals perfectly rounded breasts.

I never believed I would view a virgin as having such a *perfect* body, but fuck me, if Caterina does. Her breasts are large enough to fill my hand, and round as though constructed by a doctor. They lead into a flat stomach and toned thighs.

"Now, remove your panties."

"No."

Random acts of defiance. While they're charming, they're also aggravating.

"They come off or you don't shower."

War plays out over her expression, and I can almost see what she's thinking. At this point, there's little of her body not available to my gaze, and it's obvious by the way she looks to the glass walls at her side, she wants a shower.

An outcome too ideal to ignore. When a person desires something, it means they'll gamble all stakes against it until they get it.

Her fingers hook in the strings at her hips, and she pushes the scrap down her thighs, past her knees, and drops them when they reach her ankles. She completes her striptease by stepping out of them, nudging the thong to the side as her hands immediately cover herself, but it's too late. I've already seen what she has to offer.

"Get in the shower and clean yourself."

Relief ripples over her expression, and this time, she obeys right away. While she distracts herself with turning the hot water on and eventually stepping under the steamy stream, I undress. Piece by piece, my clothes fall to the floor. The black tux contrasts her white, silk thong, and I shove them into the same pile. After all, the groom's clothing mixes together with the bride's before he passionately takes her on their wedding night.

And she *will* receive a wedding night.

Her hands come up to her neck and she scrubs away the fucker's blood. I watch as she uncaringly uses my things without asking, Rossi's engagement ring shining from her finger. She picks up my bar of soap and begins rubbing it against the blood. She misses spots, of course.

Which is where I come in. Well-deserved, really, considering she hopped into the hot water without a backward glance. The princess should keep her wits about her when she doesn't have a bodyguard to do all the heavy lifting.

I open the glass door and step inside. She doesn't notice, so I approach, keeping only an inch of space between our bodies. Despite the hot water sluicing down, she does feel me and her head whips around, wet strands slapping me in the face.

Her mouth opens, anger lines instantly marring her face, but then her mouth snaps shut and she spins back around. There's a tenseness in her shoulders, giving away her true feelings. Of course, she chooses now to keep silent, praying I don't steal this shower from her.

"Why are you in here?" she politely asks instead.

Silently, I rest my hand over hers, pressing heavy into her until she flinches and pulls her hand away from the soap bar, leaving it in my palm. I pick up where she left off, ensuring every speck of Rossi's blood is scrubbed from her body before I replace the soap to its spot.

"You still haven't told me why you kidnapped me."

I grasp her shoulders and spin her. Water strikes the back of her head before hitting the tiled shower floor.

Caterina gasps at seeing *me*. My cock bobs partially erect between us, twitching under her gaze, and that has her lips parting—in desire or fear, I'd love to know.

"You're—what..."

For show, my hand lands on my own cock and I stroke myself once, twice, until I'm completely erect. Her skin flushes so deep, I can basically *see* the blood roaring through her body. Caterina's eyes slam shut, and she turns her face away, ever the demure one.

But this is where the fun begins.

"Caterina," I rumble. "Kitty Cat, look at me."

The nickname does something to her. She shivers before her clenched eyes relax and slowly open, careful to keep them on my face and nowhere lower.

"You're here because your father owes me something. You're collateral until I get it."

Getting the response she wanted smooths out her features and her spine straightens. She's a mafia princess through and through and understands the life. A simple nod follows, seemingly accepting my words.

"What would it take for you to return me then? Land? My father will give up a chunk of his control over the city to get me back, I'm certain. Money? He'll give you millions if you drive me home right now. I'll see to all of this."

Money and land. Caterina doesn't realize that by being the collateral, I'll get all that and more.

I think over my next words, careful not to give too much away and spoil the fun. "Perhaps, instead, I'll accept favours from you. Payment before I release you, and I'll call your father's debt paid in full." I pause, letting the words sink in, but she merely watches me expectantly. "What would you do for me?"

"Anything." The virgin in her peeks out because she has no clue what *anything* can mean.

"Hm." I close in on her, stealing the space between us, until she adds more by skittering back, pressing her back to the glass wall behind her. But I don't stop. Not until my body is lined up with hers and my cock brushes her stomach.

"What are you doing?" she asks, hurriedly, her eyes darting down and up so quickly, I'd miss the action if the entirety of my focus wasn't on her.

"You said *anything*."

Her lips part and she shakes her head to deny me, but it's too late to stop a hunter when he's trapped his prey.

My head bends and I catch her lips with my own, kissing her roughly. My tongue skirts her lips, demanding she opens up to me. After a tentative second, hers part and my tongue slips in. Hesitancy and inexperience tinge the kiss as when I take her tongue, she pulls her mouth back once before meeting my lips again, giving me control once more.

My hands fist in her hair, and using the long strands as reins, I tilt her head, ensuring she can't get away from this, from me. Not until I'm done taking. My cock twitches between us, stroking the soft skin of her stomach. I don't groan, unwilling to show her how a simple kiss has my lust skyrocketing with need.

What I *need* is to claim my crown and be done with this treacherous game.

The kiss continues, rough and ravenous, and I remove one hand from her hair to drift down her back toward the curve of her ass. My touch wakes her and her mouth rips away from mine.

"What the fuck?" Fire emerges from her soul, burning away the demure princess her parents so carefully designed. "What the fuck, Enzo? You bastard! You took my *first kiss*. It—"

I stop listening. My ears shut off in favour of reliving her previous words. *I* stole her first kiss. Virgin, yes, because it's what her family safe-guarded, but to never even been kissed before...it's a damned gift I hadn't even realized I craved.

"That was your first kiss?" I check, interrupting her ongoing bitching.

"That's what I said."

I grin, unable to help it. *I* was her first kiss. I'll be her first everything.

"You're an asshole, Enzo. That wasn't yours to take."

That's the thing, Kitty Cat. It should have been mine to take from the very beginning.

"And you said you'd do anything to return home, therefore, it's a fair price. Now that you're used to my touch, I think it's reasonable you return the favour."

Fear flickers in her gaze and tension makes her shoulders slump as she realizes her loss. "What do you want?" she finally asks.

My response is instant, driven by a deep-seated need and a growing desire to take her to new depths of degradation.

"I want you on your knees."

7

CATERINA

Girls at school once spoke of the acts they shared with their boyfriends. While I may have never kissed anyone before, I do know what one is *supposed* to do. Franco's words earlier today weren't really a shock because I'm aware of what I'll be expected to do. Expected, as is my role, but Mom claims eventually I'll come to enjoy it.

And it's not that I didn't *enjoy* Enzo's kiss, but he never asked for it. He took a first from me he shouldn't be allowed to.

Based on his words, it's obvious he wants more firsts. As long as they're not *all* my firsts. Looking at my parents after today will be hard enough, but if I return to them impure, it'll be my ruin. My downfall. Dad won't be able to find me a suitable marriage, and my entire purpose in the family will be gone because my virginity somehow makes me more valuable in dealings.

"Kitty Cat." The nickname is full of warning.

"Enzo." A lump forms in my throat and I swallow it down, before saying, "Enzo, no. Please don't."

"Beg harder, Caterina. It makes me hungry." As if to enforce his words, I spot his hand grasp his-*him*...his thing. It's large, bobbing from

48

his form, and looking entirely too foreign, despite the images and videos I once looked up. The girls spoke so highly of their boyfriends', and I was curious about what all the excitement was about. A flush travels to my thighs, and I ignore the new ache there.

"I'm serious," I whisper. "Enzo, please don't do this."

"Do what?"

He wants me to say the words. "Whatever you want, I'll do it. If it keeps my family safe and gets me home, fine. But please not *that*."

"*That* what?" His lips pull in an evil grin.

My throat burns with my rough gulp. "Sex."

"You don't want me to fuck you."

"Yes," I reply, pleased he gets it. "Please not that far."

"If you get on your knees and suck my cock, I won't."

I stare at him for the longest second, waiting for the joke to display on his expression. Nothing comes, so when I feel he'll be keeping his promise, I willingly degrade myself and lower onto my knees for a man who isn't my husband. For a man who's done nothing but bring evil in my life.

The cold tile feels chillier against my knees, reminding me of my reality. Hot water from the shower slides down my back and I watch it swirl and fall into the drain between Enzo's feet. If only it could take me with it.

"Such a pretty princess."

He's condescending, and I should despise the nicknames, but instead, my insides flood with desire.

"I didn't think I would enjoy the look of you on your knees as much as I do, but damn, Kitty Cat. How do you feel?"

"Do you care?" I snap.

"No, but it's polite to ask. Look up, Caterina. I want to see your pretty eyes when you look at your master."

Master. He's *not* my master. My thighs press together again, and I shift, my knees already sore from the hard tile.

But then my eyes lift, and I follow his instructions, realizing for now, he *is* my master. As much as the thought is unbearable, Enzo has taken me from my family and will only return me when he gets what he wants. For now, he wants me on my knees, doing the unspeakable.

His hands lower from himself. He's huge, bobbing in front of me, a mere inch from my mouth. I see now, I'm lined up perfectly.

"Open up."

I can't believe this is happening.

"Open," he demands again. "No teeth. Don't bite or I'll kill you."

He means it, most likely. Eventually, my usefulness will run out.

I part my lips. My eyes flick up to his, waiting and watching for the next step, and—

He shoves himself into my mouth, making me choke.

"Mmugh!"

"Take it like a good girl, Kitty Cat. Open wide and breathe through your nose. I'll teach you how to suck cock just the way I like it."

My hands flay, catching on his thighs, but my movements are soon ended by the hard grip he claims in my hair, twisting the strands until the burn radiates over my skull. It's easy to ignore though, in favour of the pain from stretching my mouth wide as I accommodate him.

He's the first man I've ever put my mouth on, obviously, but it's clear he's uncaring about my inexperience, as he's making it so I'm merely a wet hole for him to find his own pleasure.

He completes the circle of hell a couple more times—in and out of my mouth until his hips slow to a much more manageable pace.

"Flick your tongue on my underside, Caterina."

I do so, simply thankful his roughness seems to be over in exchange for training.

He groans, and I repeat the action, hating how instinct drives me. The throb, unlike I've ever felt before, is too aching to ignore, and I shift, my mouth tightening around him as I work into a more comfortable position—one that'll hopefully rid myself of whatever evil feelings he's brandishing inside me.

"Whoring yourself out all without direction. Such a pretty girl. Pull your lips tight and continue doing what you're doing with your tongue."

I follow his direction without question, ignoring the painful burn in my jaw. No doubt, with how wide he forces my mouth open, I'll feel this tomorrow. Still, he appears to be enjoying it with his faint noises.

"Look at me," he demands.

Can I? It seems like much of my focus is on managing my mouth, yet he wants more. I skirt the path of his body, up his toned stomach and chiseled abs, directly into my enemy's face. Lust coats every inch of his expression, and I...I like it. I *like— enjoy* this act.

The grip in my hair retightens, reminding me of his hold. With it, he yanks on my strands, continuing until my lips have no choice but to lift from his skin. His heady breaths fill the air, mingling with the pouring water still hitting my back, reminding me where we are.

He reaches past me and switches off the shower before commanding, "Stand up."

I do, my legs crying with the new position. With the water off, the air around us feels cold and unwelcoming. My arms find my body, attempting to retain some of my heat, despite the burning embarrassment at what we just did.

What *I* did.

"Arms at your side. You seem to think you can hide from me, but I won't allow it."

"What more do you want from me?"

His lips lift in a snarl. *"Everything."*

Everything. I wish I knew what he meant. His gentle allusions are nothing without a meaning behind them.

Enzo moves, towering over me and forcing my back, once again, to the glass wall. I hiss, flinching with the chill. When he advances again, his hardness between us, the cold no longer matters. Nothing does.

Nothing but the stuffy air he surrounds the room with. The stuffy air that has my lungs working hard to breathe. The very air that should continue giving me life, but rather, it pauses.

"I was your first kiss. The first man to fuck your mouth." A large hand lands on my stomach and my muscles lock, unable to move, despite the warning signs flashing over his head. The warning signs are a necessary reminder to rid the dampness between my legs.

His hand slides down, covering my mound, and I nearly yelp. The only person, other than myself, to *ever* touch me here was Dr. Zelman. The other month I had to complete an annual checkup, but it's different with her. Being a doctor with the appropriate tools and medical setting removes the intimacy.

Enzo's fingers continue, finding the spot right above my clit. My breath catches and my eyes flick to his, watching and waiting for his next move. He spreads the skin and—

"You're wet, Kitty Cat. Your pussy likes everything we've done so far."

So far. Words threatening this isn't over—that his touch isn't the end. Whatever *this* is.

When he finds my clit, I float. Jolt. Fly. All at the same time. A sound escapes my throat, but I don't recognize it.

"And now," he whispers, his face going to the space between my neck, "I'll be the first to give you an orgasm."

Two fingers circle the throbbing nub before flicking me once, then twice. The noises in my throat grow at the same time my thighs tighten, keeping his hand in position.

No, this shouldn't be happening. I shouldn't be enjoying this. I should—

His fingers shift, pausing on my core for the briefest second. I'm working on collecting enough breath to push him away when he enters me.

Bastard took...

The thought dies away as he *takes*. Takes all of me. One finger pumps inside while his thumb finds my clit again. I'm being rubbed on the inside *and* outside, and it's my body paying the price. My legs buckle into his hand, sinking him into me another half-inch. Moans crawl up my throat and my nails slam into the glass at my back, seeking something to hold onto.

"I'm the first man here, Caterina. How does that make you feel?"

"I hate you," I spit with as much venom as I can muster in between pants.

"Seems like it."

His curling lips are the final thing I see before my vision blurs and my head falls back against the wall. He's evil incarnate, seizing something not given, but more so, for taking my strength.

"Tell me, Kitty Cat, have you ever masturbated?"

My eyes fly open, and when his grin grows wider, I know he sees the embarrassing truth on my face. When the girls at school spoke about the things they and their boyfriends did during summers and holidays back home, I would imagine them at nighttime. My hand would find its way down my panties, and I'd touch myself, picturing faceless men completing the same acts with me as they spoke about.

These acts.

Then, eventually, it wasn't enough and curiosity—*what's the saying? Curiosity killed the cat. Yeah, that.* Curiosity killed me and I watched online porn.

"Hm," he hums, "tell me, Caterina, did you touch your clit?"

"Yes." The admittance is breathed with discomfort.

His thumb presses harder into my clit. "Like this?"

His touch is better, but I won't confess that. "Yes."

"Did you ever put your fingers inside this tight cunt?"

For effect, his finger pumps harder, causing the heat in my stomach to expand.

"Yes." But I didn't enjoy it. It didn't feel like the girls described; like how this feels. This is otherworldly. This is something else. This is—

My hips grind on his hand, robbing my mind, sanity, and logic in the process. The heat builds, my insides clench around his hand, locking him in me, and when his finger flicks at my clit, it's the final thing I need before I fly.

I have my first orgasm.

Because no matter how hard I tried, I couldn't bring myself to one on my own. Perhaps, I spent so much energy focusing on the imagery I needed to bring me to that point, I couldn't do it. Whatever the reason, it never worked.

His fingers pick up speed, but I don't watch. Don't care as I lose myself to everything I shouldn't be feeling. My head finds home against the glass—no longer cold against my skin—as I cry out every ounce of strength I have.

"I never thought a virgin's orgasm would be so beautiful, Caterina."

A gentle honesty fills his words, as though he spoke without wanting me to hear him.

And so, returns my sanity, and I push him away, his fingers slipping from my core.

"You're a bastard, Enzo. That also wasn't yours."

"But I stole it," he counters, deleting the space between us again. His arms cage me in, reminding me how fragile I am. "And I'm not finished yet."

Before I can wonder the meaning behind his words, his head swoops down to give one of his captivating kisses. His arms come around my body, and within a second, I'm in his arms, his still-rock-hard cock between us, reminding me where my mouth was previously.

"This is going to hurt," he whispers.

All this hurts. This beautiful betrayal pains me.

"But you're going to give me what's mine. After today, you won't be able to leave."

What does that—

Burning. Pain. Scorching agony.

One finger was fine. Two would have stretched me, and I believed he didn't try out of some fragment of decency.

But that *other* piece of him is inside me.

He's inside me.

He pumps once, twice, in and out, until my body continues its betrayal and gives him the opening to sink all the way inside and steal what most definitely is *not* his.

Me.

My virginity.

My innocence. The small piece of skin only reserved for my husband.

No one will want me after this. Perhaps this is Enzo's grand plan. Why, I can't even begin to guess.

Enzo pauses his thrusts. "The pain will pass in a moment."

He picks up his pace again, this time slower, his arms tightening around my body and ensuring I'm unable to fight this at all.

"You're a fucking bastard."

"I am," he agrees. "Soon, you'll learn why."

The he moves faster, and beneath the pain, is something else. Something I hate.

Pleasure.

Something granting him entry into my body, giving away my deepest secret. That while he's taking me without permission, my insides are enjoying this. I don't think I can come again though, but thankfully, it doesn't seem to be in his plans, since he thrusts a final time, groaning, and his release spills inside me.

No. He came inside me. Worse than a man who *isn't* my husband forcing sex onto me is him leaving his sperm behind. I'm not on any birth control, as I was expected to produce Franco's heir, which means it's possible Enzo did that exact thing.

Enzo slows. With every bit his cock softens, I harden.

With hate.

Vicious betrayal.

My arms fly, smacking him on the cheek, uncaring if he kills me after this. Better to kill me than return me to my family.

"You fucking promised, Enzo. You *promised* you wouldn't have sex with me. I'm *ruined.* But that's what you wanted, isn't it?"

Enzo lowers me to the ground before stalking from the glass shower, grabbing a towel from a nearby rack on his way past. Ignoring me isn't an option this time, so I rush after him, wet feet silenced by his room's padded carpet. Water drips from my hair and body, leaving a trail behind, my footprints imprinting on the carpeting, but a damp carpet is the least the bastard deserves.

"Now, no man will ever have me." I catch up to him, throwing my body at his until my fists slam into his back. Over and over, I hit him, uncaring what more he can do while the tears pour from me, burning my cheeks as they mix with my rage. "First my fiancé, and now *this*. *Why*, Enzo?"

Enzo ignores me, continuing into the other adjoining room. He pulls on fresh slacks and a plain shirt and spins, pushing past me again.

He's not listening. He doesn't care.

I stop at the doorway, my next words spoken with all the venom I can muster up. "Earlier today, you commented I'm no longer the child you remember. I have news for you, *Lorenzo*," I use his full name for effect, "you're not either. I never imagined such a friend would become a villain."

Enzo spins, finally giving me his attention, but it's with a look that has me shrinking back. "I'm not the same, Caterina, because this isn't a damn fairy tale. Life—this life—being a Made Man doesn't leave room for such notions. As a woman, you better learn that real fucking quick." His shoulders heave with his deep breaths. "You want the truth? If I didn't kill Franco today, eventually, you'd be a widow regardless. Because that's what this life does to people. It takes us, puts darkness in our veins, and teases us with more. So much, until we do unspeakable things in the name of getting that *more*."

I scan him, noting his tight fists by his side and the way he's no longer looking at me. His conversation began with Franco, but why do I get the sense there's more to it?

Enzo pads closer, but I don't move. I let him capture me this time, yanking me steps closer where he leaves only a small bit of space between us.

Warm breath blows over my face, masking the hate I felt for him moments ago. "You want to know why I've kidnapped you, Caterina? Kitty Cat." His throat moves with his swallow. "You were always supposed to be here. You shouldn't still be a princess because you'd be the queen. *My* queen. Our fathers wanted to bring our families together. That summer was the first of many moments we should have had. Our parents planned for summers at the cabin, winters in Aspen, and everything in between. We were supposed to grow up and be the best of friends, to fall in love in the most pure and natural way this life allows for, so when our wedding day arrived, it was a formality for the love we already felt toward one another."

Wedding day. Oh. My. God. "W-we were engaged?" I breathe. My gaze falls to the side, to Franco's ring on my finger and I imagine it instead encased with his.

"We were," he affirms. "You and I should be a damned king and queen of an empire. Today should have been about us. The dress you wore should have been for me. The aisle you were preparing to walk down would have led you to me. That ring on your finger would have been my branding. Today should have been a moment of true happiness for both of us. Caterina, I fucked you because I'm taking what is rightfully mine."

Quick, so quick, his fingers wrap around my hand and I feel it lighten as he snatches Franco's engagement ring. I don't try to stop him from stealing it. After all, what's one more thing at this point?

Enzo turns and stalks away, and by the time I recall how to breathe, he's gone.

8

ENZO

My hand tightens around the gold and diamond in my hand. It's weighty, and definitely expensive, but still an insult to give to a woman like Caterina.

Caterina is *mine*.

A quick text returns Marcus outside my door, rubbing the sleep from his eyes. After a meaningful look, I stalk away from my room, hoping that by the time I return, she'll be passed out from exhaustion, shock, and pain. I was rough with her, but I had to be. Gentle and quick don't often go together, and we'll have the rest of our lives for me to train her in all kinds of sex.

Sure, guilt is an uncomfortable bitch burning the edges of my heart, but the farther I get away from her and her supple body, the easier it becomes. Being her first time, her skills aren't the best I've had—actually, they're not even close—but I'll gladly teach her everything she'll need to know—and to train her body to crave what I'll give.

Despite it being well past midnight, I find Antonio in a sitting room, sipping something golden from a glass as he stares at a book on his lap. I recognize his expression; he's not actually reading.

I drop into the padded seat beside him. "Anything?"

He shuts the book without marking his page. "Nothing from the Bellinis. I'm surprised."

I shrug. I'm not, because Leo will exhaust every other possible lead before accusing us, aware of what incorrect blame can do.

"Doesn't matter." I mindlessly spin Caterina's ring around my pinky finger. "It'll be over tomorrow. Send a note to Bellini stating I have his daughter."

Antonio's attention lands on the ring. "Lorenzo, what have you done?"

"I ensured Leo won't prevent the empire Father once hoped for. That's all I'll say on the matter."

I walk away, leaving him to ponder those words while I catch a few hours' sleep on the couch in my office.

I'm positioned in my leather desk chair, feet hoisted on the desk's surface as I twirl Caterina's engagement ring around my pinky finger. Earlier, I replaced it with my own while she was asleep. One filled with diamonds and much more fitting for Quebec's Princess. She'll find it when she awakes, and then, perhaps, she'll piece together the missing elements from what I admitted last night.

Antonio got word to Bellini, and reports through the city have him on his way here. Guards are on standby in case he tries something, with a few specifically stationed at Caterina's door. She'll be joining us, but only after a chat and when I feel her father won't try to snatch her away.

Of course, such a blatant attempt would be to risk his own life, as well as anyone who comes with him.

A bang echoes from down the hall, followed by *"Corsetti!"* I prepare for the wrath that's about to be brought down upon me, smiling regardless.

Beside me, Tommaso shoots a worried look. He's been reserved ever since he and Antonio heard how things will go over the next hour.

Thundering travels down the hallway toward my office and a moment later, Antonio opens the door, followed by Leo and two of his own men, all apprehended by my guards. Two. Interesting number. Watching them be led in like dogs, he failed in thinking two would be suitable protection.

The door shuts behind them, and I snap my fingers—a signal to release them. My men do so right away and Leo brushes his suit jacket, casting me a venomous look.

"Was that necessary?"

"Yes."

My men form a wall behind them, blocking the door to ensure no one gets away, while Antonio stands on my other side. For all his reservations, he won't show any dissension in the ranks, not speaking or acting against me in front of Bellini.

Slowly, so drawn-out it's meant to be agonizing to my guest, I drop my feet from the desk, and straighten in my seat, palming the ring.

"If you have men readying to break in or scale the walls of my home, I warn you now, call them off or risk death. You will not be seeing your daughter until I allow it."

Leo's face flushes an angry shade of red, but he shakes his head. "I wouldn't insult you like that, Corsetti. Risking Caterina's life isn't worth it."

At least we're on the same page then. Based on his exp.ression, he's telling the truth. I gesture to one of the chairs situated in front of my desk.

"Well, then, have a seat and we'll get this over with."

When he's sitting, he mutters, "I assume you're to blame for Franco's death."

Instead of responding, I toss him the ring. Leo catches it, examining the gold in the light, gaining his answer that way.

"Am I to also presume your father informed you of the past?"

I gesture to Antonio at my left. "My uncle, actually. Franco's death was to avenge my father after *you* ordered the hit." I raise my brows, narrowing my gaze at my father's true killer. "You're fucking lucky I'm feeling generous today. You'll live—for now." Because if I kill Bellini before marrying his daughter, this plan goes to shit.

Leo's neck moves with his gulp, and he focuses on the ring between his fingers again.

"That ring is revenge for what you've taken from me. And your daughter," I smile, lips curling in viciousness, "well, she's insurance for what's owed to me."

The ring disappears in a tight fist, and he nearly leaps to his feet. Nearly, but his large stomach keeps him grounded. "What the fuck did you do?"

Instead of answering, I stand, slowly walking to the front of my desk where I prop myself on the edge. "I ensured my future wouldn't be stolen from me again. I'm renegotiating the terms of your previous agreement. After today, Caterina and I are to be engaged and wed within the month. I heard you've already decorated for a ceremony, so it won't be too much of a challenge to pull off."

"No. For the same reasons I cancelled on your father back then."

Mother's been dead for five years, and she's still a pain in my ass. "My mother was a vengeful bitch. My father claimed legitimacy of me in his will." My arms spread wide to indicate everyone in the room. "No one here challenges my claim, so you shouldn't either. The past no longer matters."

In the same conversation in which I learned about the past, I also learned why the engagement was called off. Both Mother and Father were faithless to one another. This world doesn't care what men do, but they certainly condemn women for the same actions.

When Father learned of Mother's lover, he killed him, but when he impregnated his mistress, the child—me—was claimed as his rightful heir. My mother was confined to the mansion for nearly a year, guaranteeing no one would spot her flat stomach.

According to Antonio, Mother was a willing participant. She was struggling to provide Father with a child, and she raised and loved me as hers, but never let go of the grudge. Once I reached five, she apparently reverted to the cold woman she had once been. When Father had an opportunity to further his bloodline, she didn't care, and admitted the truth to Bellini, who then called off the engagement for illegitimacy concerns.

"You're a bastard and unfit for my daughter."

Like his daughter, there is no choice here. I lean forward, putting my face in line with his. "You don't have an option. I fucked your daughter, therefore she's mine. She might be carrying my heir." Coming inside her was my insurance, because if I'm lucky, she'll be pregnant after last night.

His eyes bulge and he lunges from the chair. My men grasp Leo's jacket, throwing him back into his seat and leaving him to fume with a hated gaze.

While he's reacquainting himself with his rightful place, I text Marcus, instructing Caterina be brought down. Within minutes, there's a quick rap. I wave my hand, indicating permission for my men to open the door.

Caterina rushes in, but I don't think she even spots her father. Instead, her hand whips up and a red jewellery box flies across the room, narrowly missing my head.

9
CATERINA

After yesterday, the bastard thinks it's okay to place a fucking ring on my pillow. If he believes I'm putting it on, he has another thing coming. Its shining diamonds sparkled in the morning sun when I opened my eyes. It nearly found its way through the window but instead, I hung onto it, preferring to toss it at its owner rather than the outdoors.

What I *do* put on is the clothing he's left on the end of the bed; thankful I won't be forced to go through today naked. Dressing moves my limbs in ways reminding me of yesterday. My thighs ache from where they were stretched, my abs from the clenching, a result of the orgasm, but the central pain comes inside me, from where he took me so roughly.

I'm barely finished cataloguing my aches when the door flies open and a large man fills the entranceway.

"We're going now."

No question. Just a demand. When I approach the door, he slaps a meaty hand around my wrist and pulls me through the hall, down ornate, marble steps, then down another hallway, stopping at a simple wooden door. He knocks once before it opens.

My eyes narrow on Enzo, ignoring the many other figures in this

63

room, including my father, even though my heart leaps. Without thinking, without caring of the consequences, my arm flings back, releasing the ring box and letting it soar through the air.

It misses—*damn*—but lands on the desk beside him, where he lifts it between two fingers, his brows cocked.

"Caterina, come here."

"*Don't* speak to my daughter like that." The guard pinning Dad's shoulders tightens his hold.

I smile softly and stomp toward Enzo. For now, it's clear he retains all the power. Dad might be here but based on the small army Enzo positioned outside the room, he's still ruling.

Enzo lifts the jewellery box, lining it up with my face. "Is that how you say thank you to your fiancé?"

"My fiancé is dead," I snarl. "You're not him, and never will be."

"Seems like she doesn't want you," Dad states.

"I don't," I agree, staring only at Enzo.

He ignores both Dad and me, lifting the lid of the ring box. Between fingers much too large for the delicate gold, he removes the ring and slides it on the fourth finger of my left hand. The heavy gold, weighed down by more diamonds than my previous ring, taunts me.

"Why?" I ask, even knowing why. I pieced it together last night.

After he left, my mind recounted his story countless times. Enzo and I were an arranged marriage from childhood, but a dark past tore the deal up. Enzo continued to repeat how he'd reclaim what was owed to him, and he did exactly that. He took my virginity, ensuring I'd be ruined for another man. Future arrangements for my hand would either cost more money, because Dad would need to pay for my fiancé's silence, or would be to a lesser man. No high-ranking Made Man would want me when I was claimed by someone else. It's the way of the archaic mafia.

The rightful thing would be for him to marry me.

When I woke to find the ring, it solidified my assumptions.

"No," Dad lashes out again. "I won't play into your deceptive game.

I'll find her a perfectly respectable match." His eyes find mine, agonized, and I see the honourable fight in them. He wants to win, but he knows the life better than anyone.

"You might be carrying the next Corsetti leader," Enzo states. His hand goes to my flat stomach, reminding me of a fear I had yesterday. "I claimed your virginity, therefore you're mine. Even if your father finds you another match, I will kill any man you attempt to wed."

"No," I breathe, stepping back. His hand falls away from my body with the distance. "I'll run. Child or no child, Enzo, you're a villain. I won't live in this life with you."

He stands from his desk, towering over me. "I'm not asking, and I'll lock you in my room if I have to."

Dad stands too, the guard holding him allowing him up. Perhaps because the guard felt what I so clearly see. Perhaps because he read the room and determined my dad's defiance won't change anything.

Either way, I spot the apology. The way Dad's gaze drops to his feet and his jaw locks. "Caterina, I'm sorry. Once it gets out that Lorenzo murdered Franco and kidnapped you, and you were alone with him, the Families will assume." His attention lands on my hand—on Enzo's ring. "I can search till the ends of the earth for a respectable match, but in the end, Lorenzo has every claim on you for all the reasons he's listed. I'm sorry, honey."

This is it. Just like that, I'm engaged. Again. And once again, not to Prince Charming. It's clear now, I'll never get a happy-ever-after. Whether it be Franco or Enzo, happiness isn't in the cards.

Whatever passes over my expression has Enzo ordering, "Everyone out."

Feet rustle, but Dad's voice rises above the rest. "Until the wedding, she's my property, therefore she comes home to her family."

Property. The word hits harder than usual. It's not the first time I've been referred to by such a moniker, but it hurts more this time, for whatever reason.

Enzo peels his eyes from my face and his head turns slowly toward my father. So slowly, it reminds me of a horror movie. His voice is just as terrifying. "Caterina is *not* property. She's a fucking human, and a damned good one at that. You will treat her as such, or I will rip your heart from your chest."

I look away, uncertain who's side to take at this point. My past and future are colliding, and neither are exactly great in this moment.

"We're still enemies, Corsetti. Do not threaten me or I'll—"

"Do not threaten *me*," Enzo interrupts. "Get the fuck out of my home."

Dad isn't given another chance to speak because Enzo's guards push him from the office, Dad's men following close behind. Two older men, ones that were situated by Enzo's desk are the last ones out.

The moment the door is shut, Enzo faces me again. "I'm sorry for your father. He'll never speak to you like that again."

My arms lash out, narrowly missing his perfectly sculpted face. "You're just as bad. You fucked me simply so you'd get the life you were once promised. You both used me. I don't see the difference."

"I'm *keeping* you, Caterina. That's the difference, Kitty Cat."

But not because he wants me.

～

For the past three days, I've hidden away in his room, even locking the door, although if he wanted inside, it would be easy for him to break in. Still, it feels like I'm winning and maybe that's the reason he's allowed me to keep my solitude.

Food has been delivered at the door with only a knock signalling its arrival, but every time I open the door, there's no one hanging around. I can only assume he's instructed his staff to stay away.

This time, when the knock comes, it's not at a typical time. Standing from the bed, I slowly approach, hesitating at the last second because, no doubt, it's *him*, come to gloat.

Instead, the soft, "Caterina," coming through the wood is a voice that feels entirely too long since I've last heard it.

Uncaring if this is some trick to open the door, I throw it open, catapulting myself at Viola. My sister grins, pushing me back into the room.

"You realize how much effort it took Mom to get me in here? Your fiancé certainly has this place locked down."

The mention of Enzo wipes away my grin and I feel the second my mood drops exponentially. Backing away, I fall on the bed, crossing my arms and watching her as she scans the room, an appreciative expression on her face.

"I must admit, I'm a bit disappointed in you. Dad said you fought against Lorenzo, refusing to stay here, and all that. And yet, here you are." Her brows lift.

"Why should I run away? Where would I go that he wouldn't find me, or that our own family wouldn't hand me back to him? If you haven't heard, I'm ruined goods now."

Viola scoffs, striding forward to hop onto the tall bed beside me. Even at fifteen, she looks at me through ageless eyes, but it's what this life does to children.

"You stayed for a reason, Caterina. Locking yourself in here only allows him to win. Why?"

"I know how this will end."

"Try again. You've always spoken about your happily-ever-after with a prince. I'm starting to wonder if they exist in this life."

"I wonder that too," I murmur. "I don't think princes and the mafia go together but..."

"But," she prods when I don't finish my sentence.

I lift my head, meeting my kid sister's knowing gaze. "My version of a happy ending is simply what the marriage ended up as. I don't believe Franco would have given me one. Not in the way I'd be content with."

"And Enzo will?"

"Men take what they want, when they want it, especially if it's what they believe they deserve. Can I hate him for that?"

"Can you?" she repeats my own question.

"I guess I can respect why he did it. I don't know if Mom told you, but he and I were engaged when we were young, but it was broken off. He was always supposed to be my fiancé."

"Does that change anythings?"

"I'm not sure. I guess, whatever the outcome of my life, whether it be Franco, Enzo, or someone else, I just want to be happy."

Viola slides from the bed, standing in front of me. "I never said anything, Cat, but the few times Mom and Dad allowed me around when Franco was over, I hated how he looked at you. It didn't seem very nice."

I huff my silent laughter. Even a kid picked up on his darkness.

"I just met Enzo for the first time downstairs," she continues. "Franco seemed...mean. Enzo gave me a nice feeling."

I narrow my eyes, smirking. "Who made you the expert on who's moral or not?"

She smiles and flicks her hair playfully, batting her eyelashes. "Not sure if you've realized, but I'm getting older. Seriously," her smile drops, becoming serious again, "you said so yourself. Princes might not exist in this life, but what if you can make him into one?" When I don't respond, stunned by her thoughtful question, she backs away, waving. "See you soon, Cat. Stay in touch."

The door opens then shuts as she disappears after the most riveting conversation she and I have ever had, her words filling this room long after she leaves.

I've spent three days rationalizing his actions, and while I *hate* them and prefer to pretend I don't understand him at all, I suppose, Viola has only filled in the parts my mind refuses to. Enzo isn't Franco, and even though he stole my virginity and murdered my fiancé in front of me, I feel that over time, Franco would have been far worse.

"Princes might not exist in this life, but what if you can make him into one?"

Maybe I don't need a prince. Just some semblance of happiness.

10

ENZO

For days, Caterina has hidden away in my bedroom and I've slept in my office, far away from her. Why, I wish I knew. There's nothing but my own pointless fears preventing me from climbing into bed beside her.

There's some part of me that doesn't care about the outcome of our marriage. She's served her purpose and that's all there is to it. And yet, another piece of me wants *her* to come to *me*—not the other way around, to prove she doesn't completely despise me.

Tommaso drums his fingertips along the edge of my desk, from where he sits in front of me. "Regrets?"

I rub the ache from the back of my neck. "None."

"That's why you're sleeping in here all the time, right?"

"I'm giving her time. I did disrupt her life, after all."

His brows lift, head tilts to the side. "That's interesting. Not at all the same tune you were singing days ago when you kidnapped her from her own wedding."

I shrug, verbally admitting to him what I haven't to myself yet. "Maybe I don't want her to spend the rest of our lives hating me. At every turn, I'll fear she'll consider suicide simply to escape."

"Interesting," Tommaso repeats, this time standing. "The bit I knew about Franco Rossi says that he was a grade A ass, and had a heavy hand around women, if you catch my drift. *That* was who she nearly married. If you don't want an unhappy marriage, don't be what he was." He pauses at the door, glancing back. "Do you remember what your father would often tell you about what a leader should never do?"

"A leader never shows weakness. For a woman, for the family, for an enemy—never."

Tommaso purses his lips, nodding as I speak. "I never was fond of that saying. Because there are times one would need to show weakness, even for a woman."

With a final head tip, Tommaso exits quickly and quietly, leaving me to stare at the door, mentally repeating our conversation.

Showing weakness isn't something that comes easily to me, but I understand his words. Being vulnerable in front of Caterina may be what's required before she understands I'm not the villain she thinks I am.

Leaning back, I catch sight of a knife at the corner of my desk; the same one I used to murder Rossi and slice Caterina's monstrous wedding dress from her. For our union, she'll wear one of her own choosing, whether she likes it or not.

Step one to not being Rossi is to not shove her into something her parents believe I'll enjoy. Fuck that. I want her in something she chooses to walk down the aisle in.

And I need to inform her of that.

I'm up and out of my seat before my thought completely formulates. I rush past various staff, ignoring the head nods until I'm in front of my bedroom door. A door I'm positive is locked.

I check the knob, and sure enough, it is. Easy enough though, I pull my keys from my pocket, finding the one that'll open this door, and slip it into the lock.

I push it open, scanning the space and seeking my unwilling fiancée. She leaps to her feet, her body language indicating how unwelcome I am.

She doesn't move though, remaining in her spot as I slowly pace across the room.

"Hello, Kitty Cat."

Her nose lifts into a sneer. "What?"

"So unfriendly," I croon. With three feet between us, I stop, pulling an item from my pocket and flicking it toward her. My black credit card lands at her feet.

"Buying me won't work. That's not who I am."

"I don't need to buy you," I remind her. "I already own your ass."

"Charming." Her expression indicates I'm anything but. "I'm serious, Enzo." She kicks out at the card, only moving it a mere inch. "Whatever you think it is I want with your money, I don't."

"Buy a wedding dress of your choosing. That's what I want you to use the card for." Then I give her my back, quickly striding away.

I make it to the door before she calls out, "Wait. You're serious?"

"Very much so," I respond, turning around. "The other day I asked you if you liked the dress you had on and you said no. Too big. Not you. I agree, which is why, for our wedding, I want you to pick out your own. Don't bring your mother because I won't deal with her talking you into something else."

Caterina bends and picks up my credit card, her gaze locked on it. I wish I could read her, but she guards her emotions so well. Silence passes between us, so I open the door to leave.

As I'm shutting it, I hear her soft voice reply, "Thank you, Enzo."

11

CATERINA

We're married one week later. This time, I'm in a much slimmer dress, one I picked out myself after Enzo's visit the other day. The visit that seemed to solidify what Viola and I spoke about.

Viola stands beside me as my only bridesmaid, while one of Enzo's cousins is his best man. This wedding is much smaller than my last, with only family present.

Dad's fuming from the audience and Mom is carefully smiling, as though she's uncertain how to feel. I got a respectable match—an under-boss—but not the one they planned for, so from Mom's perspective, it's partially a win.

Enzo's hands cup my face, and he brings me closer for a kiss—the first since that day in the shower—the day everything changed. His lips are soft and unyielding, demanding my participation, and I give it. *For show*, I tell myself, but the reality is, despite everything, my body hasn't stopped burning for him.

After, Enzo and I retreat to his—*our*—room. This time, I don't fight him as he slices my dress from my body and leaves it abandoned on the floor. When I turn away, he doesn't force me to look at him.

"Caterina."

The deep desire in his tone is compelling but I don't give him an ounce of attention.

"Caterina, don't run from me. I'm tired of doing this."

I slide into bed, under the silk covers to feign sleep. "You should have thought of that before you forced me into *this*."

He sighs, a sound sticking in the room long after he finishes. "I'm sorry."

Sorry? He knows how to apologize at least. My perfectly styled hair whips around my face with the speed I sit up, focusing on his form at the end of the bed. He stares at his hand, at the wedding band I placed on his finger hours ago.

"I'm sorry with how this occurred."

Not sorry for the fact of it all but...it's a start.

"Thank you."

"I don't deserve it, Caterina, but I'm asking for you to move on. Not to forgive or even forget, but to move on. You and I are together for the rest of our lives. I promise I'll never take a mistress, and if you never want to have sex again, well, then I suppose I'll live a sexless life." Shadows pass over his expression as green eyes clash with mine, granting me a look like the first time I woke here to find him staring at me. "The lives my parents led...I don't want that. Call me a romantic," he scoffs, shaking his head at himself, "but I won't condone cheating from either of us."

"Thank you," I whisper. That possibility would make this life that much more miserable.

"I'm not a prince," he continues. "But I want to give you a happily-ever-after. I understand what I've done is unforgivable, and I'm not saying it'll be instant, but eventually, I do want us to be partners."

He heads toward the doorway and my stomach lurches with a new desire, knowing we ultimately want the same thing.

"Wait," I call out, lifting onto my knees. I hold my arm toward him, offering my own olive branch. "I hate you, Enzo, but I've also spent a week imagining you as Franco."

Enzo flinches.

"Franco felt *wrong*. He scared me, but I assumed it was because I didn't know him. When he told me how he'd take me roughly, I clammed up. When you *did* take me roughly, I enjoyed it, even when I shouldn't have." My hand still hovers, a dull ache climbing the limb as I keep it steady and waiting for him to take. "Marriage with him would have been cold. There'd be no sharing a bed. No promises to be faithful. But you...

"Enzo, I'm not accepting your apology. But I agree. You tricked me, you stole me, for the most unromantic reasons, and I hate you for it, but I want to try. If it takes ten years, so be it, but I don't want to spend the next fifty living in a hateful, loveless marriage. I've always known life in the mafia means to expect twists, and I've embraced it."

A person can only hold onto so much hate before they become depressed and struggle to find a meaning to live. It's not how I want the rest of my life to go.

The reality being, the moment I stood in front of my mirror the other week and prepared to wed Franco, I wasn't having a fairy-tale romance. It's obvious it's not something I'll get. Being a mafia woman—a daughter and wife—means to make the best of the situation. For me, it's accepting Enzo's actions. The past can't be changed, but I can affect how the future progresses.

My fingers wiggle, inviting him back to me. "Come here."

This time, he doesn't hesitate, before joining me on the bed. Rather than waiting for him to question it, my hands push at his tux's jacket, forcing it onto the bed. Then I go for his shirt, unbuttoning each one and baring more of his skin.

"Caterina." The word is dryer than usual. "You're mad."

"I want you." I peek between my lashes, amused at his reaction. "You're not quite the same man who forced himself upon me. I'm doing all the work, but isn't it your job to command me?"

His eyes darken, the light green becoming a forest at night, but still, he makes no move to react. "Only in the bedroom, and only when you ask for it."

"I want it," I breathe the admittance, recalling how all the names he called me had me wet. How, despite the situation, I *enjoyed* what he'd done.

My words unlock something in him, and he lifts from the bed before finishing his own undressing and returning to me. His body covers mine, his hands wrapping my wrists. He lifts my arms, stretching them onto the pillow above my head.

"You leave them here, or you won't be allowed to come."

My teeth sink into my lip, and I nod, staring up at the black canopy as Enzo slides down my body, readying to do whatever he—

Oh my God! The sensation, the indescribable feeling, of Enzo's mouth on my core is more than my brain can comprehend.

His tongue flicks my nub once, twice, and I cry out, hands flying to grip at his hair. The second my fingers touch his head, he lifts his mouth, halting the delicious feeling, to peer up at me. Wickedness coats his wet lips alongside my desire.

"Kitty Cat, I warned you. Hands up, or we're done."

I'll die before he ends this, so I obey. Once he sees my hands on the pillow, his head lowers again, and his tongue drags up the entire length from core to clit. My hips arch into his mouth, a moan soon following. His licks don't end until I'm screaming his name.

"That was quick," he comments. "Clearly, an act you enjoy."

"Yes." Heavy, panting breaths consume the room and I lower one hand to rest it on my beating heart. "Oh, fuck, Enzo, yes I very much enjoyed that."

"Good." Enzo leans forward and presses his lips to mine, granting some of my own taste back to me. "Because I'll happily eat you out every day for the rest of our lives."

"Let me catch my breath, and then maybe." I roll to the side, and instead of resting how I said I would, I reach for his hard cock, catching the bead of precum on his tip.

My thumb rubs the liquid around his head, faster when he groans. When I wrap my hand around his length, his hips surge. I cup his balls, rolling them.

"Kitty Cat, who's the fucker who taught you that, so I can murder him?"

"You did." And porn, but I won't mention it. "Will you come like this, or do you want my mouth?"

"Both." He grins. "But I plan on coming inside your pretty pussy because I'm going to continue filling you up until you're pregnant, like the perfect wife you were trained-to-be."

The moment he speaks like this, I lose all sense of self and want to only be a body for him. My hand tightens around him, and I increase my pumps until he pulls back and demands my next position.

"On your knees. I've been dreaming about this ever since I watched your pert ass march its way into my shower."

Not the position I was thinking, but I flip onto my knees, waiting as his fingers stroke my core, one dipping slightly in before he places himself at my centre.

"This won't hurt this time. Never again. Only pleasure for my princess."

He surges inside me, filling me. There is some pain again, leftover from my first time, but once he's seated fully inside, it evaporates in place of desire.

I rock back on my knees, but his hands on my hips stops any movement, and he takes over, controlling when he pushes inside me, the speed and intensity, and ultimately, my orgasm.

As I come, his fingers find my clit, and he rubs me into the high.

And the next high.

And the one after that.

Until, he finally joins me in bliss.

We spend the rest of the night exploring each other until I pass out beneath the power of his mouth.

Maybe I can do this marriage.

12

ENZO

For the next month, we fuck relentlessly. For someone who was a virgin a short while ago, she's taken to the life of being a king's slut, exactly as I've enjoyed becoming a queen's whore.

If this is her version of accepting my apology, I won't complain one bit.

I've never wanted a woman's love, but what I don't want, is her hate. People claim the line between love and hate is thin, but it's not. I've felt the differences and her hate is *strong*—rightfully so.

I didn't pre-plan the words I spoke to her on our wedding night; they came from the heart—from my desire to see her smile. I *want* her happy, because when she's happy, she smiles, and her smile is the most fucking beautiful thing in the world.

So, when she began undressing me, I wanted her to make that ultimate decision. And she did, giving me permission to take over and possess her in all the ways my body craved ever since tasting her first time.

God, her taste is so damned sweet with the awareness I'm the only man ever to be inside her, and somehow, it changed how she affects me. I can't count how many times I had her come on my tongue, or on my

77

fingers. How many times she willingly touched my cock, even taking it inside her mouth again. This time, with *my* ring gleaming on her finger and not that other fucker's.

And the praise kink she doesn't even realize she has, but a simple *good girl* has her instantly wet.

Even my body needs a break eventually, so instead of sinking inside her again, I lift from the bed and take her with me, straight into the shower.

Where we fuck again. *Whoops.*

But once we're dressed, I lead her away from the bedroom and downstairs, toward the furthest end of the house and the most recent addition.

"Where are we going?"

I kiss her instead of responding, weaving my fingers through hers as we head down the hallway, past the library and games room, right to the end.

"Enzo." But it's masked with a giggle. A *happy* giggle, and it shoots a light sensation through me as we stop in front of the frosted glass door.

With my hand on the handle, I pause. "Once, I met a girl who was obsessed with a pretty water fountain. She spoke of sitting beside it for hours because the sound of the gentle waterfall calmed her mind. I was fascinated with how someone could be content with sitting around doing nothing. Yet, this girl went on for an entire hour about it."

To answer her questioning stare as she continuously glances from me to the frosted glass door, I open it, standing aside for her to enter the greenhouse first.

A small-ish space, about twelve feet by twelve feet, with glass walls and a roof that looks out to the massive Corsetti lands, including the forest tucked in the back. In the centre, a stone fountain, large enough the builders were able to erect an edge for her to sit on. The small babble is the only sound as I wait, bated breath, for her to say something about the house's newest addition, but she's busy studying the space. Her attention bouncing from plant to plant; a variety of small bushes, floral arrangements, and mini trees to contribute to the soothing vibes I instructed the builders to make.

"What...Enzo, what is this?"

"Some would call it a garden," I tease, walking up behind her. I rub my hands up and down her arms as I pull her into my chest. "But I'm calling it yours. A place where you can come to, to be alone. A space completely yours and this is the one and only time I'll step foot in here, unless you invite me in."

"I'm still mad at you." But she mutters it with less power than she has in the past.

"That's fine," I tell her. "Be mad for years. That's why you have this place. Somewhere to come and curse me up and down and I won't overhear."

She huffs her laugh and finally turns to face me, but her eyes are still roaming, taking in every inch. Her mouth slightly parted in awe, and I rub my thumb over her bottom lip, making her break out into a heart-stopping smile.

"Why do I get the feeling you're seducing me?"

"Call it what you want, but it doesn't change anything happening right now."

"No," she agrees in a whispered tone. "No, it doesn't."

"Check it out," I urge, releasing her with a slight nudge toward the fountain.

She goes, bending slightly at the knees to dip her fingertips into the water's surface. It's temperature controlled so it'll never be too chilly. Her fingers draw circles in the fountain, her on the ripples.

I back away to leave her in her peace, only to be stopped by her calling my name. She sits on the edge of the fountain and stretches a hand toward me, so I immediately approach. She pulls me down beside her, droplets falling onto the back of my hand from her wet fingertips.

"Thank you for making me this. This is..." She glances away, scanning the space again. "I have no words for what this means to me. The fact you remembered something so simple from that long ago is every-thing, Enzo."

I cup her cheek, stroking my thumb beneath her jaw. "Nothing about you is simple, Kitty Cat, so of course I remembered something that makes you happy. Because this right here," one of my fingers lift to tap her face, "is what makes it all worth it."

Her hand comes up over mine. "Well, I look forward to one day showing our children this space and telling them how romantic their father can be when he tries."

"One day," I repeat, the thought suddenly making my throat tight. One day, we will have heirs. My attention lowers to her stomach, imag-ining it swelling with our child.

"Like, one day soon," Caterina continues. She weaves her fingers between mine and removes my hand from her face, bringing it to her stomach.

Her *flat* stomach.

"As in, nine months from now."

Pregnant.

"You're pregnant?" My other hand comes up to her stomach too, both cupping her body, imagining the day I'll feel a baby's gentle kick beneath the skin.

"I'm pregnant," she confirms. "I missed my period and took a test yesterday."

When I came inside her, it was to ensure that the possibility would be there, but now that it's real, I feel different. Fatherhood isn't some-thing I've ever chased. It was a fact I knew would be a part of whatever future marriage I was shoved into, because every leader needs an heir to one day replace them.

Now, I have one.

But more than that, I have a woman who cares for me.

Because as my Kitty Cat's eyes find mine, I spot what she's hiding. She's more obvious than she believes. She may despise my actions, but she also hates herself for being okay with it, because beneath the hate, pure joy and love shines brightly.

For now, she can continue to hold onto her secrets.

Shifting my hands to her hip, I haul her over my lap and cage her in, my face in the curve of her neck, my palm finding her stomach again. Our child.

I took what I wanted. Got what I wanted. When Leo passes in a few more years, Caterina and I will rule over an empire.

My methods were cruel and unconventional, but I got what was owed to me.

My arms tighten around my wife and child.

And I got more.

13
CATERINA

It didn't take ten years for me to love him.

It didn't even take me *one* year to admit it to him and myself.

Enzo bulldozed into my life, yet as I tried to hate him for it, I couldn't. Hate and love mix too closely together, and unfortunately, I found myself playing on the edge of desire.

The desire in deception.

A beautiful, dangerous feeling.

Because I realized one thing. My entire childhood, I fantasized about the Prince Charming movies and books describe; the one where he saves the princess from the villain and loves her. We never see the after though, so who know what it looks like or if they even have one? Perhaps the entire institution is a lie.

Instead, I didn't have the fairy tale romance, but I *did* have the happily-ever-after, and that's good enough for me. We rule Quebec, and eventually, Enzo became Boss of the Corsetti family. Despite my status as a woman, Enzo never left me out or made me feel as though I wasn't smart enough for the gritty, dark details of our life. We agreed not to instill the stupid values upon our children—Hawke, Nico, Rafael, and Aurora.

An unlikely alliance gets created for Hawke, but one that could prove beneficial in time. Enzo has plans for the rest of our children, but nothing in stone yet.

Enzo's methods were those of a villain's, and in the end, he never became my prince. Rather, he became my king. A king of immoral naughtiness.

Over our life, I learned something though.

Wicked is more pleasing than charming.

Read all about Enzo and Caterina's children in their own fairytale inspired romances, starting with The Hunt in Elusion, a Cinderella inspired enemies to lovers romance between Nico and the woman who deceives him. Read on for an excerpt.

Shop signed books by scanning the code below:

He takes a single step into the greenhouse, just enough for the door to shut. His electrifying energy fills the small, heated space, making it impossible to breathe. My nerves are seconds away from snapping, while also being ignited with a new vitality. I want to bolt and never look back, while also hoping he'll catch me.

Where did that thought come from?

When he speaks, it's rough but also soft, propelling me toward him. A predator's speech. One I'll imagine for the rest of my days, late at night and in the secrecy of the dark, as I picture it mumbled against my skin.

"Oh, *petite souris,* do you know what we do to people who sneak around?"

Is it possible to die this very second? I want to, but instead, I step to the side, angling myself around the fountain.

He follows, his strides bringing him dangerously close to me, leaving barely any space between us. He moved before I could make it a solid three steps toward the door. Quick as a snake, and something tells me, his bite is just as deadly.

"I-I...um." There's no rational explanation for my presence in his garden, let alone this far away from the party.

Nico lifts a single brow, waiting for me to formulate a complete sentence. "Nothing to say for yourself? You're awfully far away from where you should be. Why aren't you in the ballroom, awaiting my attention like all the other good women are?"

Good women? Is that what he thinks I should be? My chin lifts a fraction and I fight to rein in my attitude. I'm not like those simpering women in that party; I saw how they all drooled over him. Men are dangerous to allow into your life.

Stupidly, my response comes before I'm able to tell myself not to say it. "Yet, *I* have your attention all to myself. Something they'd surely die for."

When his eyes flash in the moonlight, and there's no sign of irritation at my comment, I realize how severely I fucked up. I answered his challenge instead of scaring him off.

"You are correct about that," he replies smoothly. "I'm sure if I asked any of them to, they'd drop to their knees and suck my cock, audience be damned."

Why does my body heat at the mere mention—the thought—of his cock? A tremble rolls through my form, bringing my thighs closer together, thankful for the dress and the protection it provides me.

"But my attention isn't something *you* want, am I right?" he continues.

Attention can only lead to one thing—the revelation of who I am. So no, I don't.

"What is your name?"

"A-Anna Evans." I provide the name Stefano instructed me to use.

"Hm."

That's all he says though. Nico leans back a fraction, his lips pressing together as he scans me at a torturously slow speed that makes my toes curl.

Get out of here. I've garnered too much of his attention as is, and I need to get away before he asks anymore questions.

I side-step him, angling toward the exit. "Well—"

"Tell me your *real* name."

I pause, my lie clogging my throat. *Fuck.* Of course he figured it out. In his role, I'm sure he deals with many liars and learned how to pick them out.

Nico's body heat envelops mine as he steals the distance I've managed to gain between us. I freeze, locked in place by his silent command, unable to move even as he touches me.

His fingers lightly trail along the slit in the dress, following it to my hip, and I shudder, my stupid body betraying me. His touch—a stranger's touch—shouldn't feel as nice as it does. It shouldn't make heat expand into the base of my stomach.

"Still no name? Shame."

His fingers trace the edge of my panties, his touch going near where only one man has before. And that guy, the one to take my virginity, did *not* make me shudder and shiver and sigh with the promise of what could be.

Wake up, Della. Get the fuck out of here!

"If you won't talk, then I may be inclined to show you how I treat strangers in my home." His touch lingers, pausing right over my pussy, and he presses his thumb there, enticing a soft gasp from my traitorous lips, which continue to give me away. "How I *torture* them for hours until they're begging me for relief."

"Please," I whimper, but I'm not sure if I'm asking for more or for him to free me.

"Please what?" He lowers his head into the crook of my neck, his lips dancing over my skin as he murmurs, "Please what? What are you asking of me? Do you want me to let you go?"

"No," I respond immediately, followed by a stream of mental curses for not saying what I should have. That, yes, he does need to release me.

His nose skates up and down my neck, and he inhales as a pleased groan comes from the back of his throat. He's sniffing me, but the way my body reacts—the way I jolt in his arms, legs inching apart—has me questioning my own sanity.

"If not to release you, then—" His words cut off as his fingers shift, first to the edge of my panties and then beneath the material, making me jump as his thumb skates over my sensitive clit.

Consequences be damned, I want this. Him.

Fucking the hot mafia guy for a single night rather than completing my stepfather's task is completely acceptable, right?

"You want this then?" He finally finishes his question, his finger sliding through my wet slit. Every pass he takes, I grow more damp, my body giving the truth away with every beat of my heart.

Yes. "No." Logic kicks in when the fog clears the slightest for me to recall why I'm in this predicament. I need to get Corsetti off me and run away before this goes further.

"Hm." He pulls his hand from my dress, taking away his touch, leaving my core clamping on nothing and me silently gasping, tamping down the demand for him to touch me again. "Seems you're uncertain. We might have to play a little game to help you figure it out."

ALSO BY M.L. PHILPITT

Fractured Ever Afters

A 6-book (& 2 novellas) mafia romance series of interconnected standalones based on fairytales, featuring the Montreal mafia and the New York Famiglia.

The Desire in Deception (Prequel Novella)

The Hunt in Elusion

The Craving in Slumber

The Beauty in Scars

The Freedom in Captivity

The Sound in Silencea

The Obscurity in Wishing

The Bonds in Christmas (Epilogue Novella)

The Bratva's Elite

A 4-book mafia series of interconnected standalones featuring the Russian Bratva.

Merciless Queen

Deadly Knight

Defensive Rook

Violent Pawn

Captive Writings

A new adult suspenseful romance series that progressively gets darker with each book

Ruthless Letters

Obsessive Messages

Vicious Texts

Burning Notes

Twisted Holidays

A series of dark romance holiday novellas

Silent Night

Egg Hunt

Fright Night

Be Mine

Midnight Kiss

Lucky Clover

Black Magick

A 5-book paranormal romance series of interconnected standalones featuring witches, vampires, shifters, mortals, and demons.

Dark Flame

Dark Mist

Dark Storm

Standalones

A Vampire for Christmas

Audiobooks

Silent Night

ABOUT THE AUTHOR

USA Today Bestselling author M.L. Philpitt writes both dark romance and paranormal romance. When she's not writing made-up realities, she's reading them. She lives in Canada with her four pets and survives life with coffee and an obsession with fictional characters, especially the morally grey kind. By day, she masks as a therapist.

WARNINGS

- Murder
- Kidnapping
- Blood play
- Explicit sexual content
- Non-consensual sex
- Dubious consent
- Breeding kink

www.ingramcontent.com/pod-product-compliance
Lightning Source LLC
Chambersburg PA
CBHW030010010826
48973CB00009B/2749